Jack Thornt[o]
couldn't be so [

Surely Ellie would wake up soon and realise it had all been a terrible dream.

'Oh, it's you,' she declared in her slightly husky voice, making no effort to mask her dislike.

'It's always a pleasure to see you too, Angel,' Jack drawled mockingly, at the same time allowing his gaze to rove over her in a leisurely male fashion. Something Ellie had never been aware of him doing before.

Amanda Browning still lives in the Essex house where she was born. The third of four children—her sister being her twin—she enjoyed the rough and tumble of life with two brothers as much as she did reading books. Writing came naturally as an outlet for a fertile imagination. The love of books led her to a career in libraries, and being single allowed her to take the leap into writing for a living. Success is still something of a wonder, but allows her to indulge in hobbies as varied as embroidery and bird-watching.

Recent titles by the same author:

THE PLAYBOY'S PROPOSAL
A DARING DECEPTION
THE SEDUCTION BID

A SHOCKING PASSION

BY
AMANDA BROWNING

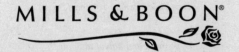

MILLS & BOON®

First published in Great Britain 2002
Harlequin Mills & Boon Limited,
Eton House, 18-24 Paradise Road, Richmond, Surrey TW9 1SR

© Amanda Browning 2002

ISBN 0 263 82925 1

Set in Times Roman 10½ on 12¼ pt.
01-0402-50163

Printed and bound in Spain
by Litografia Rosés, S.A., Barcelona

CHAPTER ONE

ELLIE Frazier was content to wait. High overhead the sky was a dazzling cloudless blue, before her stretched the sparkling azure of the sea, and the sun was warm on her bare arms and outstretched legs. Whilst the Marina Piccola, with its bristling array of yachts, bustled about her, she was happy to do nothing except soak up the atmosphere and wait for Paul to arrive.

She noted, but did not respond to, the appreciative male looks coming her way, for she was not in the market for even a mild flirtation right now, and had no wish to be approached with lines she had heard often in her twenty-six years. Without vanity she accepted that her shoulder-length blonde hair, right now hidden under a large floppy sun hat, huge grey eyes with their rim of long lashes and a generous smiling mouth drew men like moths to a flame. As did a willowy figure, with its very feminine curves, and the fact that she moved with unconscious grace. Yet it was all a matter of pure happenstance, due to her Scandinavian forebears, and she never traded on it.

There were even times when Ellie felt Mother Nature had done her a dubious favour by making her beautiful. Such as when she discovered the man she had always thought she wanted had turned out to have no heart at all. He had never loved her. Even for the short time they had been together, fidelity had been an unknown concept to him. So, after some serious soul-searching, when she realised she didn't like him anymore, let alone love him, she had ended the one-sided relationship. Which was the reason she had initially decided to boycott the family gathering at the villa on Capri this year. She had no wish to spend several weeks in his company. Now, though, she had no option. Luke had got engaged to be married, and her presence was expected.

Luke Thornton, of course, was the man she had expended so much wasted time and emotion on. He had been her idol all the time she was growing up, and now she wondered how she could have been so blind. Certain people had tried to tell her, but she had put him on a pedestal and only bitter experience had toppled him back down to the ground where he had always belonged.

He was, in fact, her stepbrother, the middle of three, Paul being the youngest at thirty, and Jack the eldest at thirty-six. Her mother had married their father when Ellie was ten. As a child, she had hero-worshipped Luke, but that had changed in her early teens to a monumental crush. She had even gone to the lengths of taking a modelling course because he was a photographer. Her adolescent heart had ached for him. She had loved him then, unquestioningly, but no longer. Thankfully her heart had only been slightly bruised, a reflection of how little she had actually loved him, but her pride had taken a knock. She had learned a hard, yet valuable lesson.

They had only been lovers for a few months, and it had been a closely guarded secret, hidden from the family. At first she had thought it was because he hadn't wanted to share her, and rather liked the spice it added to the affair. Later she realised he had a darker motive. He enjoyed doing things he knew the family would disapprove of, and they would definitely disapprove of his toying with her. Though it galled her to let him get away with it, she had no intention of revealing their affair at this late stage, for she didn't want anyone to know how stupid she had been.

It was painful to remember her foolishness. She was amazed how long a crush could last without any encouragement. Luke had never shown any sign of even noticing her, but undaunted she had stubbornly continued to love him. Going to college had opened her eyes to a whole world of young men and, though she had embraced it with youthful enthusiasm, dating and flirting and eventually having two love affairs, secretly she had been waiting for Luke, who had been off enjoying the fruits of his glittering career.

Whilst never giving up the belief that one day they would be together, Ellie had concentrated on using her talent for needlework to become a restorer, a specialist job that she took great pride in. Luke barely visited his family above twice a year, but it had been enough to keep her going. Then just before last Christmas their paths had crossed at a fund-raising in London, and her dream had finally come true.

She had looked at him and known he was seeing her at last. When he turned on the charm, she had fallen for it hook, line and sinker. They had become lovers. Luke told her then that he had always intended they should be, he had simply bided his time until she was all grown-up and away from the family. She had thought she was in seventh heaven. As she realised later, he had planned his campaign carefully, and knew how to choose the right moment.

Disillusionment had set in all too soon, but it had taken two months, and several infidelities, for her to admit he was just using her. He didn't love her. She was simply available whenever he was between other women.

That was when Ellie finally admitted to herself she didn't love him, and never had. It had been quite a revelation to realise she had been in love with love, not Luke, the man. Her pride had taken a knock, and her self-respect demanded that she put an end to the affair. She was no longer the teenager crippled by the enormity of her feelings. She was a woman who finally had the rose-tinted spectacles whipped from her eyes.

When she told Luke it was over, he had laughed and said she would be back, because she was his and they both knew it. That had shown her how he really thought of her, and it brought forth her fighting spirit. She was no man's sure thing and told him so. He had been furious. It appeared women did not drop Luke Thornton— he did the dropping. Despising him more than she thought possible, she had walked away and never looked back. Six months later, she didn't regret it. Leaving Luke was the sanest thing she had ever done.

Her hand rose to the cabochon emerald hanging from the chain around her neck, rubbing the stone like a talisman. She never went anywhere without it. It had been her grandmother's and was supposed to bring the wearer happiness in love, but it had failed her so far. She was seriously beginning to doubt there was any real magic in it.

When the news of Luke's engagement had reached her, she had been surprised. She had come to know that Luke valued his freedom too much to tie himself down to any one woman. Yet strange things did happen. Perhaps he had actually fallen in love. Whatever the rea-

son for his engagement, she had altered her plans because she knew how Luke's mind worked. He would
take her absence as affirmation that she was still tied to
him, added to which the family would want to know
why she wasn't at such an important family occasion.
So last night she had telephoned the villa, hoping to
speak to her mother.

As it happened only Paul had been home, which was
a relief because she would not have wanted to talk to
Jack, her *bête noir*, who had teased and taunted her and
refused to take her adolescent feelings for his brother
seriously. If only she had listened to him! Hindsight
could be a painful thing. Anyway, Paul had been delighted to hear that she was coming to join them, and
had faithfully promised to pick her up. Her watch told
her he was a little late, but that didn't surprise her. Paul
was a vulcanologist. No doubt he was on the computer,
logging information, and had forgotten all about her. Her
lips curved into a wry smile at the thought, but it didn't
upset her. When he remembered, he would come for her.

Ellie shifted into a more comfortable position and allowed her gaze to lazily scan the harbour, in no particular hurry to move. She had always loved this place.
School holidays had been idyllic. Endless days of sun
and sea. Later she thought it the perfect place for falling
in love. Unfortunately, it couldn't guarantee that the man
would be worth loving.

Her head jerked round as a muffled roar disturbed the
peace. An instant later a black Ferrari suddenly appeared
from one of the narrow streets and slipped like an arrow
into a parking spot across the bay. Ellie's eyes widened
as she watched the dark-haired driver climb out, removing his sunglasses as he did so and tossing them care-

lessly on the dash. It was the kind of self-possession that
expressed wealth and supreme confidence, which many
men strove for and failed to achieve. This was natural,
and undeniably alluring. Curious, she sat forward to see
him better but the distance was too great to see well,
especially in the glare of the sun and the heat haze coming off the ground.

Yet there was something about the way he stood,
hands on hips, scanning the harbour, that instantly tightened the muscles of her stomach. Perhaps it was the way
his white chinos fitted his long legs, emphasising their
powerful muscles, or the way his blue silk shirt, sleeves
rolled up, collar open, clung to his broad-shouldered
torso. Who could tell. All she knew was that everything
which was female inside her recognised a perfect male
animal with a purely primal shiver.

'Wow!' Ellie exclaimed under her breath. Whoever
he was, the man had that indefinable thing called ma-
chismo, and he had it in spades. More importantly he
was the first man since Luke who had roused a spark of
interest in her. She had begun to think herself incapable
of responding but, like one of Paul's volcanoes, it appeared her sensuality was dormant, not dead. All at once
she felt as if a dark cloud was lifted from her and she
could breathe freely again.

Unaware of her regard, the man turned away as someone called to him, then strode over to a nearby building
and disappeared inside. At which point Ellie sat back
with a bemused smile tugging at the corners of her
mouth. Strange how she had to come all this way to react
to a man again. Of course he had to have a particularly
potent brand of masculinity, in order to set her heart
racing at a distance. Whatever, there couldn't be a better

time to be having a sexual response to another man, for it proved once and for all that Luke no longer meant anything to her. Boy, did that feel good. Her response had been instant, and her body still tingled with sensual awareness.

Ellie couldn't recall having responded to any other man quite so strongly before, not even Luke. She shook her head in wonder. One glance at that man had switched her on with a vengeance, her senses leaping to attention, as receptive as the next woman to a pull as old as time.

Right then the cause of her increased pulse rate emerged from the building and, with a wave and laugh to whoever had been inside, began walking her way. Fascinated and curious, she gave in to the moment and allowed herself the luxury of watching him. Not that she could have ignored him for long anyway. He drew her eyes irresistibly with his easy way of moving. It was a walk that could only be described as catlike. Big catlike. Pantherish. With an economy of effort and yet more than hinting at leashed power. She had never seen anyone to compare with him for sheer magnetism. Definitely not Luke.

Who was this man who had the power to turn her into a seething mass of ultra-sensitive senses?

One thing was plain, she was soon going to find out. The closer he got to her, the clearer she could see him, and that was when a dawning sense of disbelief began to fill her, for she knew that face as well as she knew her own. Handsome somehow couldn't quite capture the reality of him. There was strength in the set of his chin, humour in the tiny lines at the corners of his eyes and lips. Yet there had been nothing but mockery in them for her over the years. He had been the bane of her existence. No wonder she was stunned, for it was Jack of all people she had been responding to so powerfully. Jack Thornton?

No way! Fate couldn't be so unkind. Surely she would wake up soon and find it had all been a terrible dream. Dream or not, her shocked gaze remained riveted until somewhere out of sight a motorcycle backfired, causing her to start and finally breaking the spell. Yet, when she blinked and refocused, nothing changed. It was still Jack walking towards her. It had been no dream.

Safe in the shadow of her hat, Ellie hastily dropped her gaze. Her thoughts were whirling chaotically. This couldn't be happening to her, it just couldn't. The last time she had seen Jack she hadn't experienced any of this. It had been last Christmas when she was still in the throes of her imagined love for Luke, and they had fought as usual. So what made the difference?

Whatever the cause, the result was dreadful. Thank goodness for her hat which shaded her face for she had virtually eaten him with her eyes, for heaven's sake! If he had seen that, she would never have lived it down. The only thing that mattered now was that her momentary aberration would be her secret. He infuriated her, like an itch she couldn't scratch, and the response she'd had to him couldn't be more unwelcome. Well, it was not about to happen again. The quicker she got her wayward senses under control the better.

Glancing through her lashes, she noted with a lurch of her heart that Jack had stopped a short distance away. Ready or not, she had to face him. Schooling her features into a cool mask, she raised her head, looking up at him with disdain.

'Oh, it's you,' she declared in her slightly husky

voice, making no effort to mask her dislike, and found herself looking into a pair of the bluest of blue eyes that were dancing merrily. They were, without doubt, nice eyes, and it irked her that she had to admit it. They were the sort of eyes that invited you to dive into their halcyon depths. Something she had never been tempted to do before, but now she could understand why women did. More fool them.

'It's always a pleasure to see you, too, Angel,' Jack Thornton drawled mockingly, at the same time allowing his gaze to rove over her in a leisurely male fashion. Something she had never been aware of him doing before and, to her dismay, she could only liken it to a lick of flame. As a consequence her heart knocked against her ribs in alarm. 'Why so glum? Were you expecting someone else? Sorry to disappoint you, but Luke's too busy with his fiancée to chase about after you.'

That stung, but not for the reason it was meant to do. Luke was actually the last person she wanted to see. But at least they were back on familiar ground and Ellie glared at him, thankful to be momentarily distracted from the unexpected way she was feeling. 'I wasn't expecting Luke at all. Paul said he would pick me up,' she countered frostily. 'So why are you here? Where is Paul?'

Clearly pleased with the result of his hit, Jack grinned down at her. 'He's waiting for an important message to come through, so he asked me to collect you. As I had nothing better to do, I said I would.'

She was not going to rise to the bait. She absolutely was not! 'It took you long enough to get here,' she complained, wondering how three brothers could be so unalike. Luke was the charmer—if totally insincere, Paul was endearing, whilst this man... Suffice it to say, he came from a different mould.

Those irritatingly fascinating blue eyes took on a provocative glint. 'Don't get on your high horse with me, Eleanora. I'm not impressed by tantrums. They never did work with me when you were a child, and they aren't going to work now.'

Ellie ground her teeth together in frustration. She had been named Eleanora after her grandmother, and Jack knew how much she hated it. He only said it to get her goat. She took a steadying breath and held on to her annoyance by a very slender thread. 'I don't throw tantrums, no matter what the provocation,' she responded shortly.

He laughed. 'Hmm, what a selective memory you have, Angel. A truly female trait. I could give you chapter and verse about all the tantrums you've thrown down the years.'

She just bet he could. He seemed to delight in remembering every horrible thing about her and throwing it back in her face.

'We're wandering from the point. The fact remains I've been waiting here for over an hour,' she pointed out, conveniently forgetting the fact that until a moment ago she was quite happy to sit and while away the time.

'Unfortunately Paul didn't remember to tell us you were coming until twenty minutes ago. I broke the speed limit all the way here in case you were getting anxious. Instead I arrived to find you draped seductively over the dock, wearing next to nothing, to the enjoyment of the local male population.'

O-oh. She only had to be in his company five minutes to recall why she disliked him so much. 'I happen to be wearing more than some of the women around here!' she snapped, for, whilst none of the women were actually topless, the scantiness of their bikinis meant they might as well be. She on the other hand was wearing respectable shorts and a vest-top. Modest by any standards.

Those blue eyes ran up and down the length of her, and the small smile which curled his lips was the epitome of irony. 'I thought perhaps it was for Luke. You've tried everything else, so it was only a matter of time before you got to sex,' he drawled softly and, though she tried to prevent it, hot colour stormed into her cheeks.

'I would never do that!' Ellie protested faintly, uncomfortable with the fact that Jack still believed she was angling for Luke. But she only had herself to blame for that, and for the fact that she couldn't tell him their affair was long over. So far as anyone knew, it had never happened. He wouldn't like it if he found out the truth, so she would have to make sure he never did.

Those blue eyes softened a little but still held hers steadily. 'Wouldn't you?'

'No!' she insisted, outraged at the idea, though in the back of her mind she knew as a teenager she had thought of it. At the time she just hadn't had the nerve to try it. If it came to that, she still wouldn't have the nerve. It simply wasn't in her nature. Something she felt Jack ought to know.

Jack was shaking his head disbelievingly. 'I'm pleased to hear it, even if I don't quite believe it. So, you have some other plan up your sleeve, do you?'

This visit, she realised, was not going to be as easy as she thought. Keeping up the pretence of an unfulfilled longing, was going to call for a lot of nifty footwork on a very tangled web. Somehow she must find a way to make it known she no longer wanted Luke, but without having to explain the how or why. Not an easy task. Until then she had to keep up the fiction that they had never had a relationship. So her eyes shot daggers at him, albeit not very sharp ones. 'I don't know what you're talking about. I have no plans.'

'You mean you didn't hotfoot it out here the second you heard Luke had got engaged, intent on somehow breaking them up?' Jack demanded with an icy edge to his voice that was quite unpleasant. The more so because she didn't want his brother anymore. All she wanted was to hide her own stupidity in ever falling for Luke in the first place.

'I wouldn't do that,' she denied, as forcefully as she was able, and he snorted.

'You mean you would if you could, but you're afraid you can't!' he countered scathingly, and quite without warning it brought her close to tears.

'Why are you being so horrible to me?' she charged, in a choked voice, and saw him sigh.

'Because you're a fool, Ellie, hankering for what can never be yours,' he said, with unexpected gentleness, making her throat close over.

At that moment a tiny gust of wind blew up out of nowhere and caught at her hat, whipping it from her head before she had a chance to stop it.

'Oh no!' she wailed, making a wild grab for it before it ended up in the sea. She failed, but a long arm reached for it, plucking it from the edge of the dock and an inevitable watery grave.

Jack examined his catch without amusement. 'This is

why you're a fool, Ellie. You should have let it go,' he said sternly, holding the hat out towards her.

'Why? It's a perfectly good hat,' she insisted. Retrieving her hat, she decided to hold it against further attacks from the wind.

'It's also the hat Luke gave to you,' he enlarged drily.

That sent a shudder through Ellie, because she had actually forgotten. Once it had been a precious object, now it was simply the most comfortable hat she possessed, despite the fact that it was going home. She tipped her chin up at him, aggravated that he had such a long memory. 'So what if it is?'

Jack looked her squarely in the eye. 'It's time to put away childish things, Angel. Give it up. Luke doesn't want you. He never did.'

He had no idea how right he was, Luke hadn't wanted her in any permanent sense. All he wanted from her was a willing partner in his bed. To know it was one thing. To hear it stated as bluntly as that drained the colour out of her, leaving her grey eyes looming huge in her pale face. 'You're hateful!' she gasped tightly, reacting to the remembered humiliation of admitting the truth to herself. 'You know what I think? I think you enjoy hurting me.'

There was no humour in his glance, only a steely purpose. 'Angel, the truth only hurts because it is the truth. Open your eyes and look around you. Luke may not want you, but other men will.'

Maybe they would, but the wound was too fresh. She wasn't going to tread that path again any time soon. 'I don't happen to want anyone else!' she retorted pugnaciously, aware that the statement was open to misinterpretation, but not caring. Let him think what he liked. He would anyway. Jack shook his head.

'Then you're condemning yourself to a lonely, bitter life.'

Ellie drew her legs up, wrapping her arms around them protectively. 'Maybe, maybe not. Whatever happens, it's my life, not yours. Stop telling me what to do.'

A rueful laugh burst from him. 'God, but you're stubborn!'

She shot him a scathing look. 'And you're obnoxious!' she returned smartly, causing him to grin broadly. A funny feeling settled in her chest, and she fidgeted uneasily. It was probably nervous indigestion due to their latest confrontation. He made her so mad she could spit. He ought to learn to keep his unwelcome thoughts to himself. She had enough of her own to keep her going for years to come.

With another wry shake of his head, Jack held out his hand towards her. 'Come on, let's get you back to the villa. You're tired and hungry. A rest and some good food will hopefully sweeten your disposition.'

'There you go again!' Ellie protested irritably, but nevertheless she reached for his hand and allowed him to pull her to her feet.

Unfortunately in the process she stumbled over a rope and would have fallen except for Jack's quick thinking. He gathered her into his chest, and Ellie found her cheek pressed against firm male flesh. In response to which the whole of her nervous system leapt as if she had received an electric shock, then sent tingles rippling outwards. She became vitally aware of the strength, breadth and scent of him assailing her senses. Her body seemed to go into a state of flux and, when it solidified again, nothing was the same. It was as if every atom of her being was attuned to his presence.

'Hey, are you OK down there?' Jack queried in amused concern and, still in a state of bemusement, she tipped her head up searching his face for clues to what had just happened, for she had never experienced anything quite like it.

Whatever he saw in her eyes made him go still, his own widening before turning thoughtful. For Ellie the noisy harbour seemed to fade away, leaving the two of them alone in a frozen tableau. It was the weirdest moment, and the only way she could later describe it was as if something elemental occurred leaving her feeling supercharged. She had no name for it, but it was pretty darn powerful.

'Comfortable?'

The gently ironic query brought her back to reality with a bump, to find Jack looking down at her with a decidedly rakish gleam in his eye. Immediately upon that she discovered she was still locked fast against him, and seemingly content to stay there. Shock raced through her, galvanising her into action.

'What in the world are you doing?' she gasped in a strangled voice, struggling to push him away, but they seemed all tangled up somehow. Finally, however, she was free, and stood watching him warily, breathing hard.

'Preventing you from taking an early bath,' he responded lightly, slipping his hands into the pockets of his chinos and watching her carefully.

Ellie brushed her hair from her eyes and made a meal out of straightening her clothing. Anything to give her time to get her equilibrium back. 'Thanks, but there was no need to hold on to me so long.' What was she thinking of? She could imagine just what sort of signals she had been sending out, and groaned inwardly. She had just come out of a dead-end relationship with his brother, and it was not the time to get entangled with another Thornton, no matter how he affected her.

Jack rocked back on his heels, studying her in amusement. 'Actually, I was as much held as holding,' he corrected softly, bringing her eyes back to his in a rush.

'I was not holding you, Jack,' she denied hotly, determined to deny everything, but he merely smiled.

'Sure felt like it to me.'

She found she couldn't hold his eyes and glanced away. 'Well, you were mistaken.' She hold him? She would sooner suffer the death of a thousand cuts! Good Lord, they had been at daggers drawn for years! She mustn't forget that he didn't like her.

'Hmm, I wonder if you know how revealing your reaction is?'

Oh Lord, how like Jack to make a federal issue out of it! Crossing her arms, she tapped her foot irritably. 'If it revealed how much I dislike you, then it was entirely accurate,' she returned, shooting him an icy look, daring him to continue.

Jack combed back his hair with his fingers and took her on. 'Interestingly enough, that was the one thing you didn't show.'

That was the trouble! 'Oh, well, next time I'll do a better job. Can we go now?'

'Don't you want to know what it did reveal?' he taunted softly, and she knew that whatever it was, she wasn't going to like it.

'I'm not the remotest bit interested,' Ellie asserted, bending and beginning to pick up her luggage. With any luck he would take the hint.

Jack being Jack, didn't. 'You felt it too. I saw it in your eyes.'

The simple statement sent a tremor through her system, and her throat closed over. She didn't want to talk about it, but she couldn't allow that to pass unchallenged. 'I felt nothing.'

'Liar,' came the softly goading reply and she was compelled to look at him then. 'You felt the connection, Ellie. It was like having a million tiny sparks crackling over your skin. Like it or not, it felt good to be in my arms, didn't it?'

The claim made her go hot all over, because it had felt good. Not that she would ever dare admit it. For she didn't want to feel this way about him. Their past was a battlefield. Any personal involvement was sure to be a disaster too. Knowing it, she faced him with a laugh. 'You've said some crazy things in your life, Jack, but that has to be the most ridiculous.'

He smiled with the kind of male arrogance which made her want to hit him. 'We'll see.'

Ellie's back went up at the confident reply. 'No, we won't see.'

'There's no need to be scared.'

She sent him a basilisk stare. 'The day I'm scared of you will be never.'

'I was thinking more along the lines of you being scared of your own feelings,' came his startling response, and her lips parted on a gasp.

'What do you mean?'

'That there's nothing wrong in wanting someone other than Luke.'

Gracious of him! 'I'm glad you approve,' she retorted sarcastically.

'I couldn't do otherwise when it's me you want,' he grinned at her and she blew her stack.

Of all the arrogant…! 'O-oh, that's it! Just leave it right there! You've said more than enough. I don't have to stand here and listen to it!' With gritted teeth Ellie clamped her hat on her head, adjusted her hold on her luggage, and headed off down the dock away from him. It would serve him right if she pushed him off the edge!

'Where do you think you're going?' Jack asked, easily falling into step beside her.

Ellie kept her gaze fixed firmly ahead. 'I'm going to look for a taxi.'

He laughed. 'Good luck. This is the tourist season. If you can find an empty one, I'll eat your hat.'

'Go away,' she insisted hardily, though she knew he was right. At this time of year taxis were as hard to come by as hen's teeth.

'You know, running away isn't going to change any-thing,' Jack said next, and Ellie came to an abrupt halt, dumping her bags down angrily before squaring up to him.

'I am not running away. There is nothing I have to run away from.' She couldn't make it any clearer that she wasn't interested. Why wasn't he taking the hint?

'Prove it. Have dinner with me tonight,' Jack invited, taking her completely by surprise by the change of tack.

'And risk terminal indigestion? I don't think so,' she refused point blank. It would be crazy spending any time alone with him until she had got her disconcerting re-action to him under proper control. Which, she told her-self, was just a matter of time.

'In case you're wondering, Luke and Andrea are din-ing out tonight,' Jack advised her, and she knew he would be surprised if he knew how glad she was to hear it. The longer she put off seeing Luke the better.

Ellie shrugged. 'That will give me more time with Mum and Dad.'

'Sorry to rain on your parade,' Jack interrupted without any sign of remorse. 'It's bridge night.'

Ellie glowered at him in exasperation. 'You're enjoying this, aren't you?'

His laughter admitted as much. 'You always were entertaining. So, what's it to be? Dinner with me, or an evening spent discussing the finer points of vulcanology with Paul?'

She closed her eyes momentarily. There was no contest and he knew it. Paul was a darling but… To put it kindly, sometimes his mind was a little one track.

'OK, I'll go,' she accepted grudgingly. By dinner she would have strengthened her defences anyway. She would not be giving out the wrong signals again.

Jack stooped and picked up her luggage and shepherded her towards his car. 'Gracious to the last, eh Angel.'

Ellie collapsed into the passenger seat whilst he stowed her bags in the boot. 'I know you too well to get all twittery over a dinner invitation.'

'Do you, Ellie?' Jack queried as he joined her and wasted no time starting the engine and getting them moving. 'You'd be amazed at what you don't know about me.'

She glanced at him sideways, but his attention was fully on the road. To give him his due, he was one of the safest drivers she knew.

'We've all got secrets.' Hers would send shock waves

through the family. All the more reason to keep them to herself.

'You're not interested in finding out what mine are?'

Ellie sighed and gazed out over the vista which was opening up as they climbed into the hills. 'There would be no point. It wouldn't change the fact that we don't like each other.'

'Don't we?' he challenged softly, and she glanced at him sharply.

'Are you saying you do like me?' she charged and saw him smile though he didn't take his eyes off the road.

'There's a lot to like about you, Angel.'

'There is?' she blinked, then realised how dim that sounded. 'I mean, this is such a surprise. I don't know what to say.'

His grimace told her she was overdoing it. 'Of course, it's all spoiled by this ridiculous crush you have on my brother, but you'll grow out of it.'

She inhaled sharply, thrown back into the murky waters of deception without any warning. 'There's nothing ridiculous about what I feel for Luke.' She knew how Jack would take that and he didn't fail her.

'There wouldn't be if you were ten years younger.'

Ellie turned in her seat. 'Age has got nothing to do with it. Look at you. You're, what, thirty-six now, and you're not married. Isn't that a little old to still be playing the field?'

Jack grinned as he pulled out to pass a slower vehicle. 'Not when you've found the real thing, and know you can't have it, Angel.'

His meaning took a while to penetrate, but when it

did it left her a little stunned. 'Real thing? You mean there was someone and you lost her?'

'I mean there were obstacles to our getting together. I decided, eventually, to cut my losses and look elsewhere. I'm still looking,' he explained evenly, surprising her yet again.

'Didn't that hurt?' Ellie winced sympathetically, knowing how it would have torn her apart to give up on Luke—before she realised how unworthy he was, that is.

'Thanks for assuming I could be hurt. And, yes, it did. But I wasn't going to waste my life away pining for someone I couldn't have,' he explained simply and she bit her lip.

'Like me, you mean,' she sighed, wishing his version of events was true instead of the actual reality she had lived. She had wasted so much time. Time that could never be reclaimed no matter how hard she wished.

'Don't be too downhearted. You'll see sense like I did. Then a whole world of possibilities will open up.'

Ellie shook her head vehemently. 'It's too late for that.' She had learned the lesson the hard way.

Jack steered the car into the sloping roadway that would eventually bring them to the villa. 'I'll make a bet with you that by summer's end you'll have forgotten all about Luke.'

She would never forget Luke, but not for the reasons he supposed. 'And what do I win when you lose?' she demanded confidently, as he would expect, making him laugh as he brought the car to a halt before a sprawling white stucco villa with those terracotta rooves that can only be truly found in the Mediterranean.

'Angel, if you win, you can name any prize you like.

But if I win, what will you give me?' he charged softly, but with a decided glint in his eye.

She could hardly be less generous. 'Something you want, of course.'

Reaching across, he trailed a gentle finger down her cheek to the decided point of her chin. 'I'll hold you to that, Angel,' he said with a grin before climbing lithely out of the car. 'Oh, there is one thing you should know,' he added as he opened the boot.

Ellie, who was fingering a cheek that still tingled from his brief touch, snatched her hand away and climbed out after him.

'What is it?' she asked, not quite liking the way his eyes were dancing.

'Well, when you said you weren't coming, Mum gave Andrea your room. So I'm afraid you're just going to have to use the guest room next to mine.'

He didn't hang around to check her response, for he would have known it anyway. Ellie ground her teeth together and shot daggers at his departing back. That really crowned the day. First she had found herself inexplicably attracted to the man who had been the bane of her life. Now she discovered that Luke's fiancée had been given her room. Everything was just peachy!

CHAPTER TWO

CLAD ONLY in the minuscule set of black lace underwear she had donned after her shower, Ellie padded back and forth across the cool tile floor of the guest room, brushing her hair as she went. She was feeling more than a little depressed. Her mother had barely had time for a brief chat in passing before rushing off to get ready for her bridge night, but the short time they had spent together had been worse than her meeting with Jack.

Lord, how she hated having to deceive people. Luke had never seemed to have any trouble, but she realised now that that was because he had no conscience. She had suffered agonies in the past from all the lies, and those minutes with her mother tonight had been equally painful. Ellie could still picture the scene.

Having first satisfied herself that her daughter was well, Mary Thornton had gone on in her usual cheerful vein.

'So,' she had begun, squeezing Ellie's hand encouragingly. 'How do you feel about Luke and Andrea's engagement?'

Strangely enough, Ellie hadn't anticipated that question, and her mind had floundered around for an acceptable reply before she realised that the same thing applied to her mother and Tom as it did to Jack. She needed them to know she was over Luke, without having to go into the whys and wherefores.

'Well, I was surprised, naturally, because Luke has never been a one-woman man, but to be honest, his choosing someone else didn't bother me in the least. I didn't feel even the slightest twinge of jealousy. Isn't it amazing? Whatever I felt for Luke for so long has simply disappeared. So I have no trouble at all in hoping they'll both be very happy,' she finally managed to say, and her mother had been delighted.

'That's so good to hear, darling. You know, we're glad you decided to come after all. Tom and I knew you'd see how silly you were, clinging to that thing you had for Luke. I'm so relieved it's in the past now, for your sake. You needed to move on. I had this awful feeling that you'd miss Mister Right because you were fixated on Mister Wrong. Not that Luke is really Mister Wrong, just wrong for you. Anyway, as I say, that's all past now.'

She smiled so happily, that Ellie had been unable to do more than smile back wanly. She felt more like crying. Everyone had been able to see what she had not—that Luke was the wrong man for her. Pigheadedly she had had to go her own way, and now had to suffer the consequences. It would have been wonderful to cry on her mother's shoulder, but the deception had gone on too long, and she was stuck with it. Forcing herself to be upbeat, they chatted for a while longer, then Mary rushed off, leaving Ellie to flop down miserably on her bed, her throat aching with unshed tears.

'At least I've made my mother happy,' she sighed wistfully now, fighting with a tangle that had magically appeared. 'She believes Luke is in the past, and he is. Just too late to be of any real comfort,' she added wryly.

Just then two sharp knocks sounded on her door.

'Are you decent?' Jack called out a split second before he pushed the door open and blithely stepped inside.

Shocked, Ellie stood frozen like a rabbit caught in the

headlights of a car. Jack was similarly transfixed, but only for a second. Their next actions had all the makings of a Whitehall farce. With a startled yelp Ellie remembered her state of undress and dropped the brush, grabbing up her silk robe from the bed and holding it defensively before her. Jack, meanwhile, had turned his back on her in one swift movement.

'Hey! You've got a nerve!' she charged angrily, struggling to get the robe the right way up so she could put it on.

Jack glanced over his shoulder, saw that she was in difficulties and turned back. 'Several actually,' he quipped, advancing towards her. 'All registering how good you look in black. Let me help you with that,' he offered but she slapped his hand away.

'Don't you lay a finger on me!' Ellie ordered, then blinked as he stepped back, folded his arms and closed his eyes. 'Now what are you doing?' she demanded irritably. This was so like him! He was always mixing her up, doing unexpected things.

'Closing my eyes so you can put your robe on and retain your modesty. Not that it will change anything. I've already got a perfect mental picture of you, and it's doing my libido a power of good,' he teased, making her want to hit him, though she chose to use the time more constructively and slip into the robe.

Tying the belt with hands that carried a faint tremor, Ellie walked away from him round the other side of the bed. It seemed advisable to have some distance between them. 'Do you always walk into people's bedrooms uninvited?' she charged, and Jack opened his eyes again.

'I asked if you were decent.'

'Then barged right in. You're the absolute giddy limit Jack Thornton. I could hit you!' Ellie smouldered.

'Don't worry, your revenge will come when I can't sleep tonight. Do you have any idea what the thought of you in those scraps of nothing can do to a man?' he flirted outrageously.

Actually, she had a pretty good idea. It was probably close to what having his eyes on her had just made her feel. She also knew that, now she had had time to notice, he looked incredibly sexy in his dinner suit. Scrubbed and brushed, he was more than presentable. He oozed the kind of male sensuality that scored a direct hit on a woman's senses. Hers were jangling merrily, and a wave of warmth suffused her skin. Even her breathing was a little awry.

Why hadn't she noticed this charisma before? Probably because she had never looked at him as a man before, only a pain in the neck. She was certainly seeing him now though, and the sensation it provoked was as exhilarating as it was unwelcome. She didn't want to respond to him in any way. He was the wrong man at the right time. A Thornton male, and her experience of them was not calculated to make her jump for joy.

Deciding that ignoring Jack's provocative question was the best course, Ellie folded her arms in a gesture that was half protective, half aggressive.

'OK, now that you are here, what do you want?' She got to the point and had no trouble seeing the gleam deepen in his eyes.

'You can ask that when I know under your robe is a delectably exquisite body clad only in black lace? Any hot-blooded male could tell you what I want,' he returned in a silky undertone that turned her knees to jelly and set her pulse racing.

Ellie's eyes widened at the flirtatious response. He had never spoken to her this way before, though she was used to it from other men and, whilst she was surprised, her body was registering the message on quite another level. To be blunt, it liked it.

'Be serious!' she commanded, just a tad breathlessly, hoping he wouldn't notice, but little escaped Jack.

'What makes you think I'm not?' he countered, quirking an eyebrow challengingly.

Ellie heartily wished she hadn't started this conversation, but there was no way she could back out now. 'Because you don't think of me that way.'

His lips curved. 'Don't I?'

She drew in a deep shaky breath. 'Then you shouldn't.'

'Why not?'

'Because we… That is, you and I are…' Faltering to a halt, she stared at him in perplexity.

Jack smiled, and there was no mockery in it. 'We're nothing…yet, but we will be,' he promised confidently.

Her heart lurched against her chest. 'Th-that's rubbish,' she denied, stumbling over her words, all her poise deserting her in the face of what he was suggesting.

He looked at her quizzically. 'If it's rubbish, why are you getting so nervous?'

A good question. Why was she so edgy all of a sudden? Jack had seen her in the same amount of clothes on the beach any number of times over the years. The answer was simple. Because she was now vitally aware of him as a man, and it was unsettling her, heightening her femininity. Truth to tell, she'd never been quite so aware of herself as a woman until now. There was something about the way he looked at her, so different from Luke, that was incredibly arousing. She was doing her best to ignore it, with little success. It was scary to have no control over her reactions, just when she needed to remain level-headed.

None of which she could possibly reveal to him, so she took a steadying breath and prevaricated. 'If I'm nervous, it's because you're behaving out of character.'

Both his brows rose at that. 'Is that so? Tell me something, Ellie. When did you look at me long enough to know what my character was?' he asked softly, yet with a surgeon's precision. 'No man has ever really existed for you except Luke. You've dated, probably had the odd affair, but it's all been clinical, hasn't it?'

Guilt was an uncomfortable companion, but what he said was true. The men before Luke, had simply been time fillers. She'd had no real interest in them. Until six months ago, Luke had been everything. She knew now how wrong she had been, how unfair to them. They had deserved better, and so did she.

Admitting it, though, was out of the question. Ellie tipped up her chin and fell back on the increasingly distasteful shield of her unfulfilled crush. 'I've never wanted anyone else,' she declared, and knew the instant she said it that she was asking for trouble. As expected, Jack shook his head and tutted reprovingly.

'That might have been true yesterday, Angel, but not today. Like it or not, I exist for you now.'

Her throat closed over and, shifting her weight from foot to foot, Ellie fiddled with the knot of her belt. 'You've always existed.'

Jack's smile appeared and, in a manner fast becoming familiar, her heart kicked. 'Precisely. The difference being you've seen me. There's no way back. You're aware of me, and somewhere inside you're beginning to realise you do actually want me.'

She almost laughed. If only he knew, 'realising' she

wanted him wasn't the issue. If he had been anyone else... But he wasn't, so all the more reason to deny it. 'I don't want you.'

He was less than impressed by the rebuttal. 'Because you want Luke? But he's not available, Angel. I on the other hand, would be more than willing to take his place.'

No way. Never. Absolutely not. One Thornton was more than enough for a lifetime. 'In your dreams!' she returned scoffingly but, to her aggravation, all he did was grin.

'Been there, done that.'

Ellie's jaw dropped. 'You haven't!'

The grin got broader. 'Admit it, Angel, the idea gives you a buzz.'

She stiffened in instant rejection, though in truth the thought was more than a little intoxicating. 'Not in this lifetime!'

Jack tipped his head to one side thoughtfully. 'Now what, I wonder, does that mean? That you didn't get at buzz...or that you'll never admit you did?'

Goaded, because the damn man was right...again, she shot him a snooty look down her nose. 'That's for you to decide, isn't it?'

'I wouldn't tip that perfect little nose up any higher, Angel, or you'll get frostbite,' Jack retorted laughingly, and she lowered her head with a narrow-eyed glare.

'Have you quite finished?'

He couldn't have been more amused if she had been doing pratfalls around the room. 'I wasn't aware I'd started.'

Ellie jabbed an accusing finger in his direction. 'You started the instant you walked in, you...you...' She flung up her hands in despair of finding a suitably nasty word for him. 'Ooo-ooh, damn you Jack, you are so aggravating! If you've achieved whatever it was you set out to achieve when you came here, you might as well go!'

'You know, if you weren't so predictable, I wouldn't tease you. But you rise to the bait so readily, I can't help myself,' Jack confessed in the next breath and she stared at him in something perilously close to disappointment.

'You mean this was all an elaborate ploy to get me angry? None of it was true?' A cold lump settled in her stomach at the possibility. Which was crazy, because she didn't want him to want her—did she?

'Oh, I meant every word I said,' he corrected smoothly, strolling towards her and reaching out to brush an errant strand of hair from her cheek. 'It's also trite but true that you're beautiful when you get spitting mad.'

Ellie experienced a telling burst of relief, and for a moment could do nothing but blink up at him in considerable confusion. Finally she shook her head. 'You don't think it's dangerous to get me mad at you?'

'I can handle anything you throw at me.'

Her brows rose. 'Even a knife?'

'Even that, unless your aim has improved out of all recognition. You never could throw a ball,' he agreed chuckling and, though she hadn't meant to, her lips twitched.

'I remember you tried very hard to teach me one summer,' she mused, her thoughts drifting back to a time when life had been much more simple.

'You were lousy at it. I encouraged myself with the thought that you'd be a whiz at something else. After all, throwing a ball will only get you so far,' Jack remarked wryly.

'I'm good at my job.'

Jack nodded, his mood sobering. 'That you are. I just wish you'd been that positive about the rest of your life.'

'What do you mean?' Ellie charged, frowning heavily.

'Angel, almost all your life choices have been because of one man. Nothing you've done has been because you wanted it for yourself. You've let Luke be your guiding star, but he's bound on a course you can't follow. Trim your sail, Ellie, and look around you. You might be surprised at what you see.'

He sounded so earnest, as if he truly cared about her, that she found she couldn't hold his gaze. She was sorely tempted to tell him he was right, that she'd seen sense at last, but that could lead to questions she wasn't prepared to answer. She was left only with more lies, and it was becoming an increasingly distasteful method of self-protection. Her lashes dropped to conceal her expression as she turned away. 'Why should I give up my dreams?'

Catching her by the shoulders, Jack turned her around to face him. 'Because that's all they are, Ellie, dreams. We have to have them, but we aren't always meant to see them come true. We have to change them, adapt them, and then one day what we want and what we have turn out to be the same thing.'

It was too late for that. Her dream had already come true, and it had failed her. Pride was all she had left, and it coloured her response. 'What if I can't change? What if I don't want to?' she countered as stubbornly as he probably expected and, with a flash of emotion that was hastily concealed, Jack let her go.

'Then you're a fool, Ellie. A blind, wilful fool.'

A wistful smile curved her lips. 'You'd better give up on me then, hadn't you,' she suggested, and it was balm to her wounds when Jack shook his head.

'Maybe, but not yet. Not until I've tried every possible means of saving you from yourself.'

Ellie stared at him curiously, knowing she didn't understand him at all. 'Why are you even bothering? I'm a hopeless case, you said so yourself.'

'That's for you to figure out, Ellie. If you ever do, come tell me,' he told her, then took a quick glance at his watch. 'Listen, Angel, I came to tell you I have some important phone calls to make. They shouldn't take long. I've booked the table for eight-thirty, so meet me downstairs in half an hour. That will give us time for a drink before dinner.'

He was gone as abruptly as he had arrived, leaving Ellie as unsettled as she had ever felt. If that was his intention, he was doing a grand job. She turned away from the door and, as she did so, caught sight of herself in the dressing table mirror. What she saw reflected there gave her pause for thought. There were high flags of colour in her cheeks, but she was honest enough to admit it was not brought about by anger. Neither was the sparkle in her eyes. She looked alive in a way she couldn't ever remember seeing—or feeling—before.

The why of it was vastly unsettling, and the who was nearly as bad. Jack. Annoying, aggravating Jack. She was used to him giving her a headache, but not of being so aware of him her teeth ached! He was right, he existed for her now in a way she never would have expected. Had he really dreamed about her, she wondered? Instantly she told herself not to be so foolish. It didn't matter what he had done, she was not going to get involved with him. Nothing was going to change her mind about that!

The clock in the hall chimed, startling her into the realisation that she was wasting time. Jack, no doubt, would put her lateness down to her brooding about him, which, adding insult to injury, was exactly what she had been doing. She really had to pull herself together.

Shifting into gear, she rushed around like a mini-tornado, and finished dressing and fixing her make-up in half the normal time. The half an hour was almost up as she snatched hold of her evening purse and hurried from the room. Slowing her pace as she reached the top of the stairs, she took a deep breath and made her way haughtily downwards, intent on making an impression of coolness. If she appeared remote and in control, then hopefully he would get the message that she wasn't interested. Unfortunately, when she reached the ground, Jack was noticeable in his absence, and her effort was entirely wasted.

Deflated, and secretly not a little disappointed, she folded her arms crossly. The least he could have done was be there for her grand entrance, especially as she had put so much effort into her appearance. Her make-up was perfect, there wasn't a hair out of place, and her blue dress with its tiny straps and silky fabric, which shimmered as she moved, fitted her like a dream. She had hoped to take his breath away, but instead she was left cooling her heels. How like him to demand her presence, then be late himself.

The object of her growing irritation suddenly appeared at the top of the stairs.

'Sorry I'm late,' Jack apologised with a winning smile as he descended.

Ellie was the one left looking up in awe as he jogged down the stairs with all the panache and élan of a latter-day Fred Astaire. When he reached ground level, he allowed his twinkling gaze to rove over her in lazy appreciation.

'You look good enough to eat in that dress. I'll be the envy of the whole male population.' He took her by the arm and turned her so they were reflected in a nearby mirror. 'We make a good-looking couple.'

Ellie had been thinking much the same thing. They looked sort of—natural together. A strange concept, but these were strange days. Out of the corner of her eye she caught him looking at her expectantly, and she sighed.

'OK, I'll probably have to fight off the women who want to claw my eyes out, too,' she declared grudgingly and Jack grinned.

'So you won't be ashamed to be seen with me?' he asked with a jaunty quirk of an eyebrow that made her want to grin, which was all wrong.

'Stop fishing for compliments. It's most unattractive,' she countered, not wishing to answer that. The truth was, it made her feel buoyed up inside to have him at her side. Not that she would tell him, for he had a big enough head already.

'If it's such an unattractive habit, why do women do it all the time?'

'Insecurity probably,' Ellie responded seriously, knowing it to be true in her case. 'Some women are convinced they only exist through a man's eyes.' That aspect hadn't been her problem. With Luke the fishing had been done in a last-ditch effort to hold his attention. Which was an uncomfortable line of thought, and she hastily changed it. 'Of course, there are also a lot of men who have to be coaxed into saying something nice.' At which point she couldn't resist shooting him a cheeky grin. 'They don't all have your style.'

Laughing he took her arm and urged her towards the front door. 'I learned at an early age that flattery will get me a long way. As I matured, I discovered it helps to mean what you say.'

'It got you further, you mean?' she charged drily, allowing him to help her into the passenger seat of his car.

Having taken his place beside her, Jack shot her a reproving look. 'I mean I felt more comfortable with myself.'

Ellie looked at him curiously as he set the car in motion. 'Sounds to me like you've got a bad case of integrity. Didn't it hamper your style?'

'Uh-uh. I also learned that the quality of the success far outweighed the quantity.'

Her brows rose. 'A sort of "less is more" philosophy,' she quipped, tongue-in-cheek.

His teeth flashed whitely as he grinned. 'Precisely. It's far better to like and respect the women I take out, than to see them merely as scalps on a belt.'

She couldn't help but respect him for that. Another first. His brother ought to be taking lessons from him. 'It's comforting to know you don't see me as a scalp. Do you like and respect me, too?'

'We've already established I like you,' Jack returned smoothly, taking time out to send her a smoky look.

Her heart kicked and lodged uncomfortably in her chest as she registered the deliberate omission. 'But you don't respect me?' That hurt. Far more than she would ever have expected.

'Of course I respect you, Angel. But I'd respect you more if you removed those blinkers you insist on wearing.'

So, they were back to that again, were they? Ellie thought tiredly, tensing automatically. He was like a dog with a bone, unable to let it go for an instant. 'I think we should change the subject, unless you want to be fighting all through dinner.'

'You're right. I'd rather be flirting with you than flirting with indigestion,' Jack quipped back, the remark sending a tiny frisson along her nerves.

Ellie wished she didn't find the sound of it quite so inviting. It shouldn't be. Nothing to do with Jack should affect her in any way...and yet it did. Even here in the car he was a tantalising presence. The warmth emanating from him was actually setting her flesh tingling, whilst the scent of his cologne had an allure that made her want to close her eyes and savour it slowly. It was a sensory bombardment she should be resisting, but her defences weren't co-operating. It had been a day for discovering startling things about herself, and it wasn't over yet. She didn't dare think about what the evening held in store.

Jack drove them to a popular restaurant perched on a hillside overlooking the waters of the Bay of Naples, where the food was excellent and the diners were encouraged to linger over their dinner and dance if they so desired. Ellie had never been there before, but Jack was clearly well known to the *maître d'*. They were shown to a table tucked into the corner of the terrace where gentle breezes cooled the balmy night air.

Sipping at a glass of chilled white wine, Ellie glanced around her with interest. She recognised one or two people, and exchanged smiling greetings with them, before her gaze moved on. One figure caught her eye, and she did a double take then froze, her heart lurching anxiously. Across the room, seated at a romantically secluded table was Luke. She tensed immediately, waiting for some reaction to set in. This was the first time she had seen him since their break up, and she had no idea

how she would feel. Her hand shook a little, and she set
her glass down with a tiny thump.

Jack's hand covering hers was almost as much of a
shock as seeing Luke. 'Take it easy. Relax.'

Ellie blinked at him in amazement. Relax? He had to
be joking. 'Luke's over there,' she hissed by way of
explanation, attempting to ease her hand free, but he
applied just enough pressure to keep her where she was.

'I see him,' he returned calmly.

'Well, I wasn't expecting to,' she responded testily.
This was a meeting she wasn't prepared for. Frankly,
she had been hoping to delay the moment as long as
possible.

'I thought you'd remember this is Luke's favourite
place, Ellie,' he reminded her with gentle firmness.
'Where else would he bring Andrea?' he added, and she
glanced round quickly.

A young woman had appeared at the table, and now
she and Luke were locked in rapt conversation. So intent
were they in each other, they were oblivious of everyone
else in the crowded restaurant. Jack was right, Luke
loved this restaurant. She had forgotten, but naturally
Jack hadn't. Ellie caught her breath as the implications
of what he had said struck home. No wonder Jack had
not been the least bit surprised to see his brother.
Twisting round, she looked at him accusingly.

'You knew they were here.'

'I decided it was the best way for you to see them
together,' Jack said by way of confirmation. 'This way
you can get the first meeting over away from family
scrutiny.'

Ellie groaned silently, for she knew he was right. It
would be easier to have the first meeting out of the glare
of the family spotlight. It didn't stop her wanting to hit

him for his audacity. He had no business organising her life for her.

'Don't tell me, you mean you were only thinking of me, right?' she deliberately laid on the sarcasm with a trowel. Lord, he made her so mad!

'Yes, and Andrea too, of course. Your face might have given you away, and she doesn't need to know you hate her for existing,' Jack added mockingly, making Ellie grind her teeth in exasperation. Of all the nerve!

'I don't hate her,' she denied swiftly. She felt sorry for the woman, for she doubted Luke would be any more faithful married than free. 'I don't know her,' she went on, bringing a faint smile to his lips, though not, had she looked harder, to his eyes.

'Precisely.'

Ellie allowed her gaze to stray back to the other woman. She had fashionably cut short dark hair, framing a classically beautiful face. Her eyes were stunning, large and brown, whilst her mouth was a perfect curve. She was wearing a dress that simply shrieked haute couture.

'She's very beautiful. Elegant too,' Ellie was compelled to be honest. Would looks be enough though? That was the question.

'Don't be fooled by the sugar coating. Andrea D'Abo is independent and strong-willed, not Luke's usual type of woman at all. She isn't going to put up with any of his nonsense. If he wants to keep her, he's going to have to toe the line. It's going to be interesting watching the relationship unfold,' Jack responded with amusement, drawing Ellie's eyes back to him.

She had never been able to make Luke toe the line, and Jack was implying that he expected it would be so. 'You don't think I could do that?' she just had to ask.

Jack took a sip of the manhattan he had asked for. 'Andrea is in a league of her own. You're as different as chalk and cheese. You'll never be cold-blooded enough to do what has to be done to bring Luke to heel, Angel. You're far too passionate for that. Which is fortunate, because I never have cared for insipid women.'

The implied criticism of Luke's fiancée surprised her. 'Is that how you think of Andrea? Don't you like her?'

He smiled grimly. 'Frankly it's impossible to like her. She's only interested in what will make her look good. She knows what Luke is, and yet she's determined to have him because he's the flavour of the month. Luke wants her because she moves in glamorous circles. He's willing to suffer a woman who will stand up to him and rein him in, for the kudos of rubbing shoulders with the great and good. They make a perfect couple. They're both so shallow they will probably be blissfully happy. But to answer your other question, he never needed someone who would let him use her emotions against her.'

Ellie's chin dropped, her eyes widening at the accurate description of both herself and his brother. 'Are you saying I'd do that?' She couldn't believe he saw her so clearly. It was painful to think she had been such an open book. A book he had read so very easily.

This time the smile glittered in Jack's eyes, along with something else that smouldered away in the background. 'You're far too passionate for your own good. You'd give your heart completely, and a man like Luke would break it.'

It was as if he had been there and seen it. 'How can you know that? You can't know that!' she exclaimed faintly.

'I can, because I know my brother and I know you,

Angel. You have untapped fires inside, fires Luke isn't interested in. I, on the other hand, would like nothing more than to be engulfed by those fires. Going up in flames with you would be a hell of an experience.'

Ellie felt herself growing hotter by the second as Jack elaborated on his theme. He was so right. Luke's use for passion was as a source of immediate sexual gratification. Jack, on the other hand, seemed to be saying that passion was something to be explored and shared. Something to be developed so that it would satisfy the soul as well as the body. He wouldn't leave a woman feeling used and incomplete. He had too much respect for them. More to the point, this was what he was saying he wanted to share with her! His openness was as shocking as it was arousing and, cheeks flaming, she glanced around to check if anyone had heard him.

'It's OK,' Jack reassured her coolly. 'Nobody can hear us. The restaurant it planned so that people can have intimate conversations.'

Ellie took a much needed sip of her own drink. 'That may be, but I didn't come here with the intention of having an intimate conversation with you, Jack Thornton,' she pointed out in a forceful undertone. She felt as if the whole situation was rapidly getting out of hand. She needed to bring it within bounds she could control as quickly as possible.

He laughed softly. 'Intentions have a habit of re-arranging themselves to suit the situation. For instance, you intended to make a serious play for Luke, but now you won't.'

She bridled at the unfounded charge, but at least it had the desired effect of slowing her pulse down. On this subject she knew where she stood. It might be shaky ground, but she was familiar with it. 'Even if what you say is true, and I'm admitting nothing, how can you know I won't?'

Blue eyes looked steadily into hers. 'Because you've seen them now with your own eyes.'

The statement forced her to drop her eyes. Oh, hell. He was crediting her with integrity, and under the circumstances she wasn't sure she warranted it. Had the situation been what he thought it was, that she still hankered after Luke, she wasn't sure what she would have done. Still, it made her feel better to know he thought she had goodness of spirit. Through Luke she had lost sight of what good qualities she possessed. Perhaps Jack was right, and she wasn't such a bad person for being such a fool.

She sensed him waiting for her response and sighed. 'You know, I'm fast coming to the conclusion that love stinks!' she declared gloomily, taking another larger sip of wine.

'Only the unrequited kind,' Jack corrected softly.

That brought a crease to her forehead. 'How would you…' She broke off as she remembered. 'Oh, yes. The mysterious love of your life. Was she beautiful?'

'She's not dead,' Jack pointed out with a quirk of the lips. 'She's as beautiful as ever.'

Ellie blinked in surprise as she read between the lines. 'You still see her?'

His smile was wry. 'Occasionally.'

'How do you stand it?' If she had still loved Luke, seeing him and Andrea together would have torn her apart, so she could easily imagine his feelings.

Jack's answer was surprisingly matter-of-fact. 'It isn't as if I have an option, Ellie. Neither do you. You have to deal with it and move on.'

'Be adult about it, you mean,' she grimaced, knowing she had been far from that in the past.

'If you have any pride and self-respect, you'll never let them see how much it hurts. If you're willing to grin and bear it, I'll help you,' he offered, causing her to frown.

'Help how?' she asked suspiciously.

'Well, now, the easiest way to show the world you aren't interested in Luke, is to show an interest in somebody else,' he enlarged, with just the merest hint of a gleam in his eyes.

Her heart took a crazy leap in her chest as she had no trouble at all following his line of thought. 'You're volunteering to be that someone, I take it?'

His smile broadened. 'It would be no hardship. We're already attracted to each other.'

'I do wish you'd stop saying that!' Ellie complained, not needing to hear again what she knew all too well, and got a wry shake of the head for her pains.

'You might not wish to hear it, but wishing won't change the facts, Angel.'

'That doesn't alter the fact that it's a preposterous idea,' Ellie declared roundly. 'Besides, you're no substitute for Luke,' she added for good measure. She had to put an end to this now.

Something flashed in and out of Jack's eyes and was gone before she could pin it down. 'I don't intend to be anybody's substitute. The situation calls for some defensive action, and I'm offering my services. Don't refuse the offer out of hand. Think about it.'

'I don't have to think about it, Jack. I'm not interested. There's an old saying about frying pans and fires, you know.' If Luke was a dyed in the wool rat, what did that make Jack? No, she wasn't about to make the same mistake twice.

Blue eyes danced as he watched her disgruntled display. 'Except you were never in the frying pan. Fires, on the other hand, can be cleansing and bring new life.'

Ellie's lips twisted. On the contrary, she could tell him things about frying pans he had never imagined! As for fires... 'They can also destroy. I'd rather not risk it.'

'Even if I promise not to let anything bad happen to you?' Jack wheedled with a look that sent a shiver along her spine despite her best efforts to remain immune.

'I've a feeling your definition of bad and mine differ greatly,' she returned drily, and he laughed.

'The offer remains open, nevertheless,' he said as he handed over a copy of the menu. 'Come on, it's been a long exhausting day, and you need time to regroup. Get some food inside you, and give your brain a rest for a while.'

Ellie thought of refusing, but it *had* been a long day and, despite everything, she was hungry. So she would do as he suggested, but nothing was going to make her take up his other suggestion. She might be an idiot, but she wasn't a fool. Getting entangled with Jack for whatever reason would be a big mistake. Because she was attracted and, in her vulnerable state, she might do something she would live to regret.

Besides, she wasn't in the market for another man, no matter how attractive he was. She might have broken with Luke, but that didn't mean she had to accept the first consolation prize that came along. Even if that prize brought her senses alive in a way they never had been before.

No, she was going to get through this without Jack's help.

CHAPTER THREE

ELLIE sighed appreciatively and drained the last of the coffee from her cup. She felt much more relaxed now. Jack had been a surprisingly easy dinner companion, keeping the conversation flowing with consummate ease. It was surprising how similar their likes and dislikes were. She had never noticed before. He had a wicked sense of humour, too, and had made her sides ache from laughing several times. Quite unexpectedly, she had enjoyed herself. Life was full of surprises.

Now she came to think about it, she hadn't looked at Luke and his fiancée once during dinner. Truth to tell, she had actually forgotten they were there. An unexpected but very welcome result.

She glanced their way now and felt nothing. She still despised Luke, but none of the emotions she had thought she might experience were present. Surprised, she stared at him hard, probing old wounds, trying to rouse some emotion, but nothing came. It occurred to her that, for the first time in as long as she could remember, she was totally free of him, and it felt wonderful.

'It gets easier,' Jack remarked conversationally from across the table, and she jumped, coming out of her mood of introspection.

'I'm sorry, what did you say?'

'I said it gets easier,' Jack obligingly repeated, and she realised he had mistaken her absorption for some deeper emotion.

As well he might, for how many times in the past had she insisted she would love Luke for ever? Believing she still felt that way, he would expect her to declare herself heartbroken. It was so far from the truth, she felt more than a little guilty for misleading him. Unfortunately, she recognised she was now in a hole too deep to get out of with any dignity. There again, dignity be damned. She should make an effort to put some of the record straight. There were too many lies. At the very least she should attempt to make him understand she no longer wanted Luke. That he could stop worrying about her.

'Listen, Jack…' she began to say, but got no further.

'I know it's small consolation right now, but you're doing the right thing,' he told her approvingly, and she wished he would stop being so nice because it was making her feel more and more guilty.

Which in turn made her snappy. 'Will you please stop going on about it!' she pleaded in desperation. 'I've accepted the situation, and there's an end to it!'

Those expressively mobile brows rose in mocking arcs above his eyes. Then he was pushing back his chair and holding out a hand to her. 'You're still getting used to the idea right now. Come dance with me and take your mind off it,' he suggested, yet managed to make it sound more like a command.

Ellie bridled and stayed where she was. 'I don't feel like dancing right now,' she refused, but that only made him walk behind her and start to pull her chair out. She had two choices: go with him, or suffer the indignity of landing on her behind in a public place. 'All right, all right, I'll dance,' she conceded, rising quickly.

Jack tucked her hand into the crook of his arm. 'Sensible of you to change your mind.'

'You wouldn't care if I was suffering the torments of the damned, would you?' she accused him, whilst keeping a smile plastered to her face for the benefit of anyone who might be watching.

'You can sob into your pillow all night, Angel, but right now you have things to do,' Jack informed her ominously, and she glanced up at him quickly.

'Things? What things?' she demanded to know, and had her answer when Jack halted beside Luke's table. Ellie ground her teeth in annoyance, realising she should have known Jack wouldn't let the matter rest until he felt satisfied.

The couple glanced up. Luke didn't see her at first because she was standing slightly behind his brother. A smile broke across his face as he rose to his feet. 'Jack, what are you doing here?'

'I took Ellie to dinner as it was her first night here,' Jack informed him, moving just enough for his brother to see her. Luke turned her way, the smile freezing on his lips. He looked about as pleased to see Ellie right now as she was to see him.

Like the charmer he was, though, in a flash his smile became as warmly welcoming and impersonal as ever. 'Hey, Funny Face, how are you?'

The old nickname was a pointed reminder to remember her place in the scheme of things. It angered her, but she was not about to let the cat out of the bag for her own reasons. So she hid her dislike behind a polite smile. 'I'm fine, thanks, Luke. In fact, I couldn't be better.' It wouldn't hurt to let him know she was well and truly over him.

Luke's eyes narrowed for a moment before he grinned. 'Glad to hear it. You haven't met Andrea yet, have you?' Without waiting for a reply he turned to his fiancée. 'Darling, this is my little stepsister Ellie. You remember, I told you all about her.'

I bet you didn't tell her about us, Ellie thought waspishly. Honesty was not Luke's long suit. 'No, I haven't,' she agreed, with a polite smile, and didn't miss the assessing look the other woman gave her.

Nevertheless, Andrea held out her hand, albeit with a put-upon smile. 'Don't worry, he didn't tell me anything bad. I'm pleased to meet you at last, Ellie,' she greeted politely as the two women shook hands. It wasn't lost on Ellie that Andrea broke the contact swiftly.

'Luke always did know how to keep a secret,' Ellie responded slyly, and felt rather than saw both men look at her sharply. She could understand Luke's sudden anxiety, but hadn't intended to arouse Jack's suspicion. 'Congratulations on your engagement. I came as soon as I heard.' She included the pair of them in her blandest smile.

'Jack said you would,' Luke rejoined with a laugh, and Ellie caught the glitter of annoyance in his glance. She ignored it, for the time was long gone when Luke's disapproval could tie her stomach in knots. Instead she shot Jack a dry look.

'Well, we all know Jack's never wrong,' she said with heavy sarcasm.

'It's my most endearing quality,' he returned smartly, and she couldn't help but laugh.

'That doesn't say much for the others, does it?'

'You'll be sorry you said that later,' Jack countered

with a decided gleam in his eye that made her nerves skip about.

'Won't you join us?' Andrea invited, although Ellie could tell it was merely a polite gesture, she didn't really want them there. They didn't fit into her scheme of things. At the earliest opportunity she would probably insist on Luke going to the States with her and, from Ellie's point of view, that wouldn't be a bad thing.

Jack shook his head. 'We wouldn't dream of intruding. Besides, we have plans of our own for tonight. We're about to hit the dance floor. Ellie expressed a wish to dance, and who am I to deny her,' he declared seductively, and Ellie caught her breath at the message he was deliberately sending the other couple. He was pairing them up when it was far from true. To underline the words, he slipped his arm about her waist possessively.

Luke noted the manoeuvre, and sent her a speculative look which she returned boldly. Though he said nothing, she could tell he was not amused. It pleased her to annoy him. 'Ellie always could wind us around her little finger,' he finally said with a scowl.

'If that's true, why are you marrying Andrea and not me?' she teased him immediately. She felt Jack tense beside her, but it wasn't *his* reaction she was interested in, only Luke's.

'Because I love her,' Luke declared, staring down into Andrea's eyes, believing as he did so that he struck Ellie's pride a cutting blow.

Had she still believed herself in love with him, the confession would have been crippling. As it was, it still had the power to make her wince. One thing was very clear. He was still angry with her for ending the affair.

Luke was a bad loser, and she would do well to remember it.

Even so Ellie knew she couldn't let it pass unanswered. 'Perhaps we can get together whilst we're both at the villa, Andrea. I can let you in on a few things you ought to know about him,' she suggested provocatively. 'I could tell you things that would make your hair curl.'

'How sweet, but I'll pass, thanks,' Andrea said with a laugh definitely lacking in humour. 'I'm not all that interested in Luke's past,' she added and Ellie discovered that Jack was right, it was hard to like her, even on so short an acquaintance.

Fortunately they parted on that note, and Ellie allowed herself to be shepherded to the dance floor where they joined several other couples. Jack turned her into his arms and began to guide them around the floor.

'That was a downright sneaky thing to do,' Ellie complained, holding herself stiffly in an attempt to keep some necessary room between them. Not an easy thing to do when Jack held one of her hands against his chest, and his free hand sat in the small of her back. It was generating a disconcerting amount of heat which was slowly coiling its way along her veins, draining her of the energy needed to keep him at arm's length.

'I know, Angel, but unpleasant tasks should be done quickly,' Jack explained his actions logically, but Ellie wasn't to be so easily appeased.

'Hah! You mean you didn't trust me not to cause trouble!' she charged scornfully.

'Women who fancy themselves in love are apt to do ill-considered things.'

'I never fancied myself in love with Luke. I did love him,' she insisted. It wasn't love now, but she had believed it was before she had come to her senses. She had thought she would love him for ever, but she saw now he wasn't *the* one. She had been blinded by his glitter of false gold, so that now she didn't know if she would recognise the real thing if it did come along. Not that she was looking.

'Whatever that is, it doesn't appear to have affected your appetite,' Jack returned sardonically, and she shot him a frosty look.

'I was hungry.'

Looking down into her angry face, his lips twitched. 'You don't think you shouldn't have been?' he teased her, and she felt a childish urge to stamp her foot.

'I think...'

Whatever her thoughts were, they remained unspoken for more couples had joined them on the small dance floor, and someone bumped into her back, propelling her into Jack's body. His arm closed around her instantly, holding her tight as he deftly swung them out of the way.

'You OK?' he checked as soon as they were in a less populated area.

Ellie swallowed hard and nodded, very much aware that the whole of her body was now pressed along the whole of his, and that one powerful male thigh was brushing between hers as they continued to dance. The arm she had used to brace herself away from him had somehow taken to clinging round his neck, bringing her cheek into the curve of his shoulder. Speech was beyond her as her senses were bombarded with highly charged signals which set her pulse racing like crazy.

Lord, but it felt amazingly good, was the thought uppermost in her mind. Which was why, instead of immediately breaking free, she had a strong desire to press herself closer and prolong the moment. The softly sensual brush of their bodies as they danced was doing crazy things to her insides, starting up an ache deep within her. It was powerful and heady, and for one wild moment drove all other thought from her mind. Her fingers automatically tightened on the cloth of his jacket, and for one satisfying heartbeat she relaxed against him, drowning in the spell cast by her senses.

Until a gap in the dancers gave her a fleeting glimpse of Luke and Andrea, reminding her of where she was and who with. She stiffened up immediately. This was not supposed to be happening. She was not supposed to be turning to jelly in Jack's arms—and liking it!

'Jack!' His name snapped out in an imperative undertone as her attempt to pull away was countered by strong male arms.

'What is it, Angel?' he murmured, running his hand gently down her spine, in such a way as to make her want to purr not scratch.

'You can let me go now,' she insisted, fighting the lunacy of it.

'Now why would I want to do that, when I've actually got you where I want you?' he charged drolly, and she rolled her eyes helplessly. She was neatly trapped and they both knew it, for, apart from causing a scene which she was loath to do, there wasn't much she could do if he wouldn't let her go.

She fell back on an old defence. 'Do you know how much I loathe you?'

A soft laugh escaped him. 'Your message came through loud and clear. Unfortunately it's got a little mixed now. Was that you really, really hate me, or you really, really want me?'

Colour flooded her cheeks, and it was small relief that he couldn't see it. 'You are the lowest of the low.' So she had given in to temptation for a second; he hadn't had to mention it.

'I'm glad we got that cleared up,' he declared with a husky chuckle, raising her hand to his lips and pressing a lingering kiss to her palm.

A tiny shock wave ran through her, closely followed by a curling sensation that she all too easily recognised as pure sensual pleasure. 'What are you doing?' The challenge came out in a croaky hiss. Where was her vaunted control when she needed it so badly? She had to stop this right now, or... Or Lord knows what stupid thing she might do next.

'Just what do you think I'm doing, Angel?'

The muscles of her stomach clenched as a ripple of desire fanned out to touch every nerve in her body. 'Y-you'd b-better stop it,' she stumbled over the command, for the touch of his lips was threatening to buckle her knees.

'Anything to please a lady,' he acceded, and abandoned her palm only to draw one finger into his mouth and tease it with his tongue.

That curling warmth began to spread through her system at the delicacy of the caress. 'Cut it out, Jack!' she ordered, angry with herself that she sounded more breathless than determined. Yet how could she help it when he was devilishly good at what he was doing.

Raising her head the better to emphasise her point, she found herself caught in the beam of a pair of gleaming blue eyes.

'Coward,' Jack taunted, bringing her chin up.

'People are watching us,' she pointed out desperately, but it only deepened the gleam in his eyes.

'All the more reason to carry on. This is your opportunity to show the world you're footloose and fancy free.'

She wasn't falling for that. 'All you're doing is giving Luke the impression that I'm involved with you!'

'Wouldn't that be better than to let him worry that you're still not over him,' Jack remarked, and she frowned, caught unawares by the implication.

'What do you mean? Luke's never shown I existed,' Ellie countered quickly. She should know, she'd spent years trying to gain his attention. So far as the family were concerned, she never had. Or so she had always thought, until Jack shook his head.

'Just because he never showed it, didn't mean he didn't know. He simply didn't want to hurt your feelings by a blunt rejection.'

Ellie thought she must surely have misheard, and searched his eyes to check for mischief. There was none. A cold lump of anger lodged in her stomach. There was only one way for him to know that. 'Are you saying Luke talked to you about me?' she asked, each word enunciated with care.

'To all of us. It was some time ago. You remember, when we were all home for Christmas. He wanted our opinion on what he should do,' Jack acknowledged and, had it been anyone but Luke they were talking about, she would not have thought it odd.

'And what did you tell him?' she asked, keeping her voice as neutral as she could, whilst inside her stomach roiled. That Christmas he was talking about was when they had just begun their affair.

'I advised him to wait and see. He was hoping—as we all were—that you'd grow out of it.'

It was hard to proceed as if nothing was wrong, when she was so very angry inside. How Luke must have laughed in private. Whilst she had been covering their tracks, he had been discussing her with his brother, getting his sympathy—and all the time he had known the true nature of their relationship. How he must have delighted in the danger of it, all the while laughing up his sleeve. How could she have ever thought she loved him?

'I had no idea,' she mumbled in total honesty.

'Like I say, he didn't want you upset. The point is, Mum and Dad think you have grown out of it, but Luke isn't so sure. He hasn't seen you for a while, so he's hoping you could have come to your senses. It's up to you to convince him.'

Ellie glanced away quickly lest he see her reaction. Damn Luke and his manipulations. He didn't believe she was over him, but not in the sense his brother took it. He believed she would come running at the snap of his fingers—because she always had in the past. Well, he was very much mistaken. She had twenty-twenty vision where he was concerned. Convincing him wouldn't be easy, especially as she still wanted to keep their affair a secret. A shame, because it would do her the power of good to slap his face—hard.

'I thought I just had. I gave him my blessing just now,' she argued through a tight throat. 'What more should I have to do?'

'You know as well as I do, Angel. The only sure way to convince him that you see him only as a stepbrother,

is to show a healthy interest in another man,' Jack re-
iterated.

'I doubt if I could be convincing,' Ellie muttered qui-
etly. She had never felt less romantic. Murderous came
closer to the mark.

'We'll work on it. It's a truism, but practise does
makes perfect.' Jack quickly put in, and her lips twisted
wryly.

'What makes you think I'd choose you for the task?
There are other men around.'

'But I'm the only one here,' he pointed out, eyes
dancing.

'You're forgetting Paul,' Ellie countered with a lift of
her chin, but Jack laughed.

'It has to be believable, Angel. Nobody's going to
think you've suddenly developed an interest in Paul.' He
shot that down. 'Don't get me wrong, Paul's a nice guy,
but the only passion in his life right now is his beloved
volcanoes.'

Sadly true, she concurred silently. 'The same applies
to you. Everyone knows I dislike you. We've fought like
cat and dog for years,' she was quick to point out.

Jack ran his thumb over her bottom lip. 'Love and
hate are two sides of the same coin. Nobody would bat
an eyelid. My guess is, they're more likely to nod sagely
and say they knew it all along.'

The soft caress sent a disproportionate amount of tingling through her system, and she pulled away, annoyed
that she couldn't control it. 'They're never going to believe I've fallen in love with you just like that!' she
argued triumphantly, but Jack wasn't put off.

'We're not talking love here, just attraction. A powerful sexual attraction that overrides past antagonisms. That they will believe, for one very good reason.'

Ellie's mouth went dry, for she knew the answer as well as he did. 'And that is?'

'There is a strong attraction between us, and if we act upon it, we would certainly be convincing.'

It would be pointless to deny it, and it would certainly put a dent in Luke's overwhelming ego, but... The snag was keeping control of the situation. How did she put up a convincing performance and not get caught up in the passion of the moment? She couldn't help feeling that in two seconds flat of them starting, the performance would become reality. However much she might enjoy it, and her senses were telling her she would, she didn't want to get involved with him.

'Hmm, I still think it would be better to find another way.'

'You can set the rules,' Jack put in temptingly, and she looked up at him with a wary frown.

'Meaning?'

'Meaning it will be up to you how far this attraction between us goes,' he enlarged, and her eyes narrowed again.

'Somehow I don't get the feeling you'll give up so easily,' she mused, and he grinned.

'I don't intend to. You set the boundaries, Angel, but I reserve the right to try and persuade you to change your mind.'

Now that sounded like Jack! 'I knew there had to be a catch! I don't trust you.'

Jack shook his head. 'It's yourself you don't trust. Say no and mean it. That's all you'll have to do.'

Easier said than done, if her responses so far were

anything to go by. Not a comfortable thought. It was all too much for a tired brain. 'Look, if you've achieved everything you set out to do, can we go now?' Ellie proposed, stifling a yawn that welled-up from nowhere. The exertions of the day were catching up with her—fast.

He took a glance at her tired grey eyes, and instantly stopped dancing. 'You're about out on your feet, aren't you? Come on, let's get you home.'

Jack made short work of paying the bill and collecting her purse, then they were heading out into the cooler air of the car park. It had the effect of clearing some of the cobwebs from her brain, but for reasons best left alone she didn't remove her hand from Jack's steadying arm. When they reached the car, she looked at the sporty shape quizzically.

'Isn't a Ferrari a bit ostentatious for a banker?' she asked goadingly, and he quirked an eyebrow at her. 'I mean. It has to make one wonder where the money came from, and that could open a whole nasty can of worms.'

'For your information, the car's rented,' he informed her repressively, but Ellie wasn't to be put off just yet.

'I suppose that's more your style,' she mused, 'but why a Ferrari?'

Jack released her and folded his arms. 'Perhaps it's got something to do with the fact this is Italy?' he suggested tolerantly yet warily.

'Ye-es, but why not choose a Fiat? No, I think you chose a Ferrari because it's part of a fantasy. It makes me wonder just what goes on in that head of yours,' Ellie mocked, eyes dancing with mischief.

His lips twitched. 'Stick around and you'll find out.'

Her eyes rounded. 'Am I in this fantasy too?'

'Wouldn't you like to know,' Jack teased back, then his gaze drifted past her, and what he saw brought a smile to his lips as he looked at her again. 'I thought you were tired,' he pointed out, and she sighed.

'The air woke me up.'

'Good,' Jack declared, reaching for her waist and pulling her up against him. 'I want you working on all cylinders right now. Kiss me,' he ordered, and brought his mouth down on hers.

Shock held Ellie where she was initially, but it was the sensory pleasure the touch of his lips created which kept her there, and set her hands lifting to his shoulders to cling on for dear life. Her eyelids fluttered down, and a soft sigh escaped her lips. The brush of his lips was magic, so soft she barely felt it and yet her whole body was caught in the spell. Every atom of her being wanted to know more, and the stroke of his tongue along her lips had her melting against him, her lips parting to allow him entrance.

What happened then was a slow ravishment of the senses. Sparks were ignited and coaxed into fires by each foray of his tongue. Ellie was helpless to do other than respond, joining him in a lazy, sensual dance which was all the more powerful for its restraint. She could never have imagined a kiss could be so enticing, and she gave herself up to the enjoyment of it. As her hands slipped about Jack's neck, her fingers tangling in the hair at his nape, his arms closed around her, pulling her close until not even a breath could pass between them. Passion flared, but it was slow and sultry, making their blood zing, never getting out of control whilst all the while threatening to.

Only the need for air made them draw apart, and Ellie

stared up at Jack in wonder, her heart still pounding. Jack held her gaze, and even in the darkness she could see the banked fires in his eyes.

Ellie gave her head a tiny shake. 'There must be something wrong with me.'

'You look OK from where I am.'

'I should be pushing you away.'

'Deep down inside you don't want to.'

She let that pass, and her silence was acceptance of the truth of what he said. 'Where did you learn to kiss like that?' she queried huskily, not caring that she sounded more than a little awestruck.

Jack laughed softly, running a finger gently across her tingling lips. 'Just natural talent. You were pretty awesome yourself.'

Her lips curved softly. 'I think I was inspired,' she confessed wryly.

'There was a lot of inspiration floating around tonight. I told you we'd make an explosive combination.'

Ellie might have enjoyed their kiss, but she hadn't totally lost her senses. 'Is this where I'm supposed to say, OK you've convinced me, we'll go with plan A?'

'Clearly not,' Jack grimaced, easing her away, not releasing her until she was steady on her feet. 'Believe it or not, that was light years from my mind when I kissed you. On the other hand…'

Lights illuminated the area around them as a car swept past and out onto the road.

'On the other hand, never look a gift-horse in the mouth,' Ellie finished for him, taking her eyes from the departing car and staring him out. 'That was Luke.'

Jack smiled wryly and rubbed a finger along the ridge of his nose in a gesture she knew well. It always meant he had been found out. 'They followed us out,' he admitted. 'It seemed too good an opportunity to miss.'

'How did you get to be so sneaky?' she demanded, though not as angrily as she should have. It was hard to appear affronted when she had enjoyed every second of what had just passed between them, no matter why it happened.

'I grew up with an expert at it,' Jack replied, bending to open the car door for her. Holding it, he glanced at her expectantly.

Ellie obediently climbed into the car, but she was frowning. 'What do you mean?'

'Luke always managed to get what he wanted one way or another,' Jack announced as he joined her and started the engine. 'He knew what to do and what to say, and most importantly, how to wait. As a consequence, he was rarely, if ever found out.'

Ellie stared at him silently as he reversed the car, then turned and headed home. That description fitted Luke to a tee. It was, after all, exactly what he had done in order to get her into his bed—and keep her there. Fortunately for her, she found him out, and it swept away the blinkers she had been wearing for years.

'To look at him you'd think butter wouldn't melt in his mouth,' she said distastefully, and Jack spared her a look.

'You don't sound surprised.'

'Actually, I'm not,' she confirmed, then sighed. She was tired of defending the indefensible. It was time to make another attempt to set the record straight. 'Listen Jack, I don't expect you to believe me, but I haven't been wearing those rose-tinted glasses for some time,' she added, feeling the need to prove that she wasn't a total fool where his brother was concerned.

'No? That wasn't the impression you were giving earlier,' he reminded her, and Ellie knew she would never have a better opportunity to tell him she was over her crush, and still keep her secret.

'I know, but you made me angry, so I decided to let you get on with it,' she told him sardonically.

'Let me get this straight. You're now saying you don't want Luke?' he charged doubtfully.

Ellie kept her eyes on the road ahead as she answered. 'I haven't for some while.'

'This is a very convenient change of heart,' he responded suspiciously, and Ellie shrugged.

'Come on, Jack, you're hardly the first person I'd tell. Look at today. The minute you saw me you were off again,' she reminded him caustically.

Jack was silent for about a minute or two, considering her comment. 'If it's true, then I'm glad to hear it. There might be hope for you yet, Angel.'

Trust him to keep doubting her, but at least she was making progress. 'Of course it's true. If you hadn't been so annoying, I'd have told you sooner.'

'As a matter of interest, just how long were you going to let me keep on thinking the way I was before letting me in on the secret?' he demanded to know, and she laughed.

'Hard to say, you were enjoying it so much.'

He harrumphed, but only said, 'Do the parents know?'

'Yes.'

'So now all we have to do is convince Luke.'

Ellie's nerves jumped. 'Surely that isn't necessary. He has Andrea now, and if I show no interest in him whatsoever, the effect will be the same,' she countered, knowing where his thoughts were heading.

'You can try it, if you think it will work, but my way will be better,' Jack pointed out softly.

Better for whom? Jack had another agenda, but she didn't intend to be part of it. 'Don't think this is getting you anywhere. Just because I don't want Luke, doesn't mean I'll turn to you instead!' she warned him off.

'But it doesn't mean you won't,' Jack responded with what sounded to her like satisfaction.

Ellie felt satisfied too, up to a point. At least Jack now knew how things stood. That was about as good as it was going to get. She might wish she could wipe the slate clean, but knew it was impossible. All she could really do was learn from her mistakes. Which meant not jumping straight into another one. Tempting as Jack was, she had to be sensible for once. Which was a shame, because that kiss… She sighed, knowing she was doomed to relive it many times in her dreams.

CHAPTER FOUR

NEXT morning Ellie was lounging in the doorway which led from the breakfast room onto the terrace, sipping at a delicious cup of coffee, when she heard footsteps behind her. Glancing round, she smiled as Luke's fiancée entered the room. She received a cool smile in return, and realised she was probably wasting her time. Andrea was elegantly dressed in white capri pants and a pure-silk red blouse, with not a hair out of place. Ellie herself had plumped for her favourite khaki shorts and a mini-mal vest top. When on holiday she simply wanted to relax, and fashion was the last thing on her mind. Andrea clearly had different standards. Nevertheless, she was prepared to be friendly towards her.

'Good morning,' she greeted the other woman cheer-fully. 'I thought I was the last to come down.'

Andrea shot her a cool glance as she poured herself a cup of coffee from the pot on the table. 'You are. I've been up for hours, but I have a rigorous fitness pro-gramme that I follow, and I won't miss it even if I am on holiday.'

Ellie knew she was supposed to have been put in her place, but refused to go. She shuddered delicately. 'That's far too strenuous for me, though I jog when my work schedule allows.'

'I'm trying to get Luke to join me,' Andrea confided as she joined her, looking out at the view without any show of enthusiasm for the dramatic beauty of it.

Ellie almost choked on a mouthful of coffee, and took a gasping breath. 'Good luck!' she declared with heavy irony. To her knowledge Luke had never done one exercise in the whole of his life.

'Why do you say that?' Andrea charged sharply, frowning, and Ellie sent her a sympathetic look.

'Because Luke's indolence is legendary. Now if you want someone to work out with, Paul's your man.'

'Thanks, but I'm rather choosy about my exercise partners. I have to know they're on the same level as myself,' the other woman responded, and they fell silent for a moment, studying the view of sunlight on the distant sea. 'God, what do people do on this rock for entertainment?' Andrea asked after a while and Ellie shot her a puzzled look.

'Just about anything you can do anywhere else, and it's warmer too,' she joked.

'I'm sure that's fine for the tourist, but what about those of us who are used to a higher standard?' Andrea charged with a tiny shudder of distaste that set Ellie's hackles rising.

'Actually, most of us consider the standards are high here,' she returned just a tad frostily, and Andrea shrugged.

'Really? Oh well, I dare say a few days won't matter.'

Silence fell again and Ellie made no effort to break it. From her brief acquaintance with the other woman she knew they would never get along. Luke was more than welcome to her.

'That was some clinch you and Jack were in last night,' Andrea remarked a few minutes later, sending a tremendous jolt through Ellie, who had not expected it.

Ellie turned and stared at her, colour slowly rising into her cheeks. 'I…er…'

Andrea laughed, patently enjoying her confusion. 'Lord, you're embarrassed. How quaint. I only mentioned it because Jack always seemed a little reserved—until last night. I don't think either of you would have heard a bomb go off right beside you. Though perhaps next time you should choose a place a little less public for that kind of thing.'

Ellie found herself itching to slap the other woman—hard. Instead she smiled mockingly. 'We'll try, but when the urge strikes…you just have to give in to it, and things can get a little out of hand. You know how it is.'

Andrea's lips thinned. 'I'm glad to say I don't,' she denied with a delicate shudder. 'However, if you enjoy being manhandled, I wish you joy of it. I'll say no more. Except that Jack's…nice. You could do worse.'

Nice wasn't a word Ellie had ever used in connection with Jack, but considering it now, she realised that Andrea was right. For the most part, Jack was nice. He was kind, thoughtful and generous as a rule. Only in his dealings with her had he been nasty and scathing. It was something to think about, but not now, for someone else entered the room and both women turned.

It was Luke. Andrea looked inordinately relieved and went over to him. Ellie held back, choosing to watch him kiss his fiancée over the rim of her cup. He made quite a show, and Ellie couldn't help thinking that it was for her own benefit. To remind his ex-lover what she was missing. He missed the mark by a long way.

Unimpressed, she turned her back on them. Down below Paul climbed the path up from the pool and, catching sight of her, he waved a greeting. Ellie grinned and waved back. As he disappeared round the side of the villa, a hand came down on her shoulder. She jumped like a scalded cat and looked round hastily. Luke stood behind her, and they were alone in the room.

'Where's Andrea?'

Luke set his other hand on her other shoulder and smiled down at her. 'Gone to get ready. We're going into Anacapri to do some shopping. It's good to see you, Funny Face.' He lowered his head as if to kiss her, and Ellie jerked her head aside swiftly, shrugging out from his loose hold.

'You can't just kiss me whenever you feel like it, Luke,' she declared frostily, putting distance between them.

'Why not? As I recall, you used to like me kissing you,' he argued with a lecherous look that he fondly thought was alluring.

Ellie suppressed a shudder of distaste. 'Yes, well, that was before I grew more discerning.'

Luke advanced on her, smiling and shaking his head. 'You don't mean that. You still want me. You're mine, Funny Face. You've always been mine.'

She held up a restraining hand. 'You couldn't be more wrong. I'm not yours, and I don't want you.'

He laughed. 'Liar. You couldn't wait for me to touch you. You were insatiable. A real tigress. You'll be back.'

Ellie ground her teeth in impotent anger, stunned by his overweening ego. She didn't want him, and the more he said, the more she wondered how she ever could have. What did she have to do to make him understand it was over?

'Don't count on it,' she warned by way of a start.

A scornful look entered his eyes. 'Of course I'm

counting on it, because you love me, Ellie. Everyone knows it. Come back where you belong.'

Ellie set her empty cup down with a bang and squared up to him. 'Listen to me Luke, and try to understand. I do not belong with you and I do not love you. It's over.'

To her chagrin, he laughed again. 'You're saying that now because of Andrea, but you'll soon change your mind. You'll be back. I know you. All I'll have to do is snap my fingers.'

Ellie closed her eyes, choked with impotent anger. It was like talking to a block of wood. Nothing she said got through. But he was wrong. She was not his to command and, if words did not convince him, then that only left actions.

When she looked at him again, her expression was icy. 'You don't know me at all, Luke. You never took the trouble to find out, but I'm learning about you all the time, and I don't like what I see. Dream on if you must, but you'll never have me again.'

Luke was about to argue, but they both heard light footsteps echoing across the hall. Andrea was returning, and there was one thing both Ellie and Luke had in common. Neither wanted the other woman to know about their affair. Ellie made a play of refilling her cup, whilst Luke went to meet his fiancée.

'Ready, darling? Good. I know the perfect little restaurant where we can get the finest seafood for lunch. How does that sound?' he said caressingly as he slid an arm about her waist.

Andrea looked from one to the other as if she suspected something had been going on, but merely smiled. 'Sounds good.'

'See you later, Funny Face,' Luke called out as they

left, and her lips tightened into a grim line the second they were out of sight.

Not if I see you first, she thought ferociously. She abandoned the coffee she hadn't wanted anyway and braced her hands on the table, striving to regain her temper. What a slug! How had she ever let him touch her? She had to have been out of her mind. Thank goodness she'd recovered. Dealing with the fallout was proving more of a problem, though.

Of course, she had the answer to her problem—if she dared accept it. Jack. Not that she really had a choice. It was Jack or nothing, and nothing wouldn't work. So she would have to take him up on his offer, but make sure he understood it was not for real. It would at least raise her another notch in his estimation. She would, after all, be doing what he wanted, putting Luke's mind at rest. Boy, if he really knew what Luke was thinking, he would blow a gasket. But she would do just about anything to get Luke off her back. Desperate situations called for desperate measures. Now all she had to do was find him and set things in motion.

Which proved to be easier said than done. A search of the house failed to turn him up but fortunately she bumped into Paul on the landing and he sent her off to the pool. As she approached the pool area through its concealing barrier of shrubs, she caught sight of Jack's sleek tanned body, clad in only a brief pair of black trunks, cutting through the water with apparent ease.

She was smiling reminiscently as she walked round to where loungers had been set out. Jack was a natural in the water, and could churn out lengths tirelessly. He had taught her to swim, and she had felt totally safe in his hands. Strange, she had forgotten that once they had been far from antagonistic towards each other. She and Jack had been at loggerheads so long, it was like another lifetime.

However, as Ellie looked down at him, her smile slowly faded. Muscles rippled with each easy movement, and the water flowing over his back outlined every rise and fall of solid male flesh. She remembered that kiss they had shared last night, and the feel of his strong body pressed to hers. The same body which was within touching distance and had barely a stitch on. Her senses registered all this in an instant, and her mouth went dry. A frisson swept across her skin as she acknowledged that she wanted to touch him. Wanted to find out if his body was as smooth and silky as it appeared.

Desire, hot and powerful, ignited and pulsed through her system from its source deep within her. Ellie had never experienced a need so strong, had never been aroused by simply looking at a man. It was almost scary, and most definitely exciting, but not the reaction she wanted to be feeling if she expected to keep any form of control of the situation. Perhaps it would be better if she waited to speak to him when he had more clothes on.

Good idea, she thought, and turned to leave.

'Looking for me?'

Ellie looked round hastily. Jack had stopped swimming and was resting his arms on the edge of the pool. As she watched, he flicked back his wet hair in a casual gesture that should not have been sexy, but certainly was. In the next instant he was levering himself up out of the pool with consummate ease. As he walked towards her, she was presented with a perfect view of his bronzed figure, made all the more spectacular by the water trailing off him.

How come she had never noticed he had such a magnificent physique? Because, as Jack said, she hadn't ever seen him. She was seeing him now, all right, and scarcely knew where to look. She found his chest far too fascinating for her blood pressure, but dropping her eyes presented her with a far greater problem. Ellie decided that had she had a collar, she would definitely be hot under it. As it was, she was simmering.

'What did you want to see me about?' Jack enquired as he halted a scant few feet away, hands resting on his hips.

It proved incredibly hard to gather her scrambled thoughts together and, when she did, she had to clear her throat and lick her lips in order to speak. 'I…er…came to tell you plan A is on after all,' she croaked out, and Jack's brows rose questioningly.

'Really? What happened to change your mind?'

The truth being out of the question, Ellie quickly invented a logical reply.

'I've been thinking about what you said, and saw the sense of it. It would be better for all concerned that Luke has no doubts.'

Jack combed his fingers through his hair, and muscles rippled tantalisingly. 'Ah, the voice of sweet reason, hmm? I had no idea I was so persuasive. You seemed pretty adamant last night.'

She hadn't had that conversation with Luke, then. 'I was, but like I said, I've thought about it and I think you're right. Luke needs to know he doesn't have to worry about me. Pretending to be involved with you, will put his mind at rest.'

She didn't like perpetuating Luke's lie that he was concerned about her, but when the only way to disprove it was to confess the affair between them, she had little choice.

'And when do you want our little charade to start?' Jack queried, with a strange glint in his eye that set her nerves jangling the second she saw it. He was up to something. She would bet her bottom dollar on it.

'Luke and Andrea have gone shopping, so...'

'Then that's where we'll go,' he interrupted. 'The more they see us together, the more convinced he'll be.'

Ellie had been about to suggest waiting until later, but she could see his point. The sooner the better worked well for her too. She wanted Luke to get the message loud and clear.

'OK. I have to get a present for them anyway.'

'Sure you weren't subconsciously hoping you wouldn't have to buy one, Angel?' he taunted softly and she shot him an acid look.

'Actually, I wasn't intending to come here at all, so a present was the last thing on my mind,' she pointed out tartly but, as usual, Jack wasn't about to be won over that easily.

'Something changed your mind?'

Ellie sighed. 'I realised my non-appearance would look odd.' And send Luke entirely the wrong message.

Jack's lips twitched. 'So here you are, about to embark on a love affair with me.'

Her chin went up. 'A pretend love affair,' she corrected firmly. 'You said I could set the rules, remember?'

'Ah, but where does pretence end and reality take over?' he teased with a soft laugh, which sent a shiver through her system. 'Perhaps we should put it to the test, hmm?'

Had she moved quicker, she probably would have avoided him, but other factors were at work here. She was fighting an inner battle as to what would be best and what would be good. And, as everyone knows, she who hesitates is lost. Jack had no trouble capturing her and pulling her close. A hand in her hair angled her head for his kiss, and then his mouth took hers.

There was nothing languid about this kiss. From the first brush of lips, heat expanded outwards, consuming her, and her lips parted on a tiny gasp. That was all Jack needed to claim her mouth, his tongue demanding a response from hers which he got instantly. Ellie moaned as he ravished her senses, returning each stroking caress with mounting passion.

His mouth left hers, but only to plunder the sensitised skin below her ear. Ellie shivered in reaction to the scalding brand of his lips, and her head fell back, allowing him access to the sensitive chord of her throat which he was quick to accept. It was like drowning, and her hands clung on to his shoulders as the only stable thing in the turbulent waters of passion.

Then it was over, as quickly as it started. Jack groaned as he raised his head, at the same time pressing her head into his shoulder. Disorientated though she was, she felt his heart thudding as wildly as her own. For sheer eroticism, she had never known a few minutes like it. Had Jack not stopped, she doubted she would have. Above her, she could feel his cheek pressing against her hair, then he took a deep breath and eased her away from him.

There was no laughter in the eyes which held hers,

but an intensity she somehow couldn't look away from. Her heart lurched.

'Real or pretend, Ellie? You tell me.'

Oh, it was real. Very real. How could she pretend otherwise. This attraction between them was expanding out of all proportion. How could it get so hot so quickly? It was like a forest fire ignited from a single spark, which created a fire that consumed everything in its path.

'I'd like to say it was pretend, but I'm not that good an actress,' she finally admitted gruffly, for what was the point of lying? He knew.

Her answer brought a faint smile to his lips. 'Thanks for the honesty.'

Taking a deep breath, Ellie eased herself away from him. 'This changes nothing. I still won't get involved with you, Jack.'

'We already are involved, Angel. What we're doing now is sorting out the degree of involvement. I'm prepared to compromise—for now,' he told her blithely, and Ellie gritted her teeth.

'Maybe you are, but I'm not,' she argued, and he shook his head, laughing softly.

'It always was all or nothing with you, wasn't it, Angel?' Jack responded gently. 'Speaking as someone who has suffered the nothing, I'm looking forward to the all.'

Ellie shook her head helplessly. He made it sound as if an affair between them was a foregone conclusion. However, she knew how strong emotions can play you false, and she wasn't entering into another relationship in a hurry. 'You could be in for an awfully long wait.'

Far from being put off, he shrugged. 'No matter. I'm a patient man.'

Her chin rose a notch as that struck a nerve. 'Something you and Luke have in common!' she retorted swiftly, reminding him of what he had said last night.

Jack went still, and there was no amusement in his face now. 'When it comes to our dealings with you, Angel, Luke and I are not a bit alike. Remember that.'

Her eyes widened. 'You make it sound important.'

Reaching out, he ran a finger gently over her lips. 'Oh, it is. Very.'

Something in the way he said it made her heart skip a beat. It was almost as if he were telling her something, but she couldn't quite grasp the meaning. 'I don't understand you,' she confessed with a frown that he smoothed away with his thumb.

'Do you want to?'

Did she? Would it help to know what made him tick? Was it necessary to the fiction they were about to create? Certainly it was no to the latter, but for the rest...

'Yes, I do,' she replied honestly, for Jack was proving to be a mystery she wanted to solve.

'Then we're making progress.'

Ellie waited for more, but he remained silent and her brows raised. 'Is that all you're going to say?'

Jack grinned and turned her back the way she had come. 'For the moment,' he confirmed as he fell into step beside her and they began to walk back to the villa.

'O-oh, you are so aggravating! What do I have to do, ask questions?'

'Fire away. I promise to answer them as honestly as I can,' he invited, slipping an arm across her shoulders. 'Of course, to really understand a person, you have to spend time with them. Get to know them.'

'Unfortunately I don't have the odd twenty or so years

to spare,' Ellie retorted, very much aware that his close-ness meant their thighs brushed with every step they took. 'Would you mind removing your arm. Nobody can see us.'

'I know, but this has nothing to do with anyone else. I happen to like touching you. Your skin is as smooth as silk, as soft as velvet.'

And his voice, Ellie added silently, was as seductive as thick, dark chocolate. Sinfully sensuous—and not necessarily good for you. The trouble was her senses weren't as cautious as her brain, and they responded, setting her pulse beating a little faster, and thickening the flow of blood through her veins.

She groaned inwardly, doing her best to ignore the curling sensation in her stomach. 'The idea was that this was for Luke's benefit,' she argued staunchly, and could sense the smile that spread across his face.

'True, but if we don't want the act to look stilted, then surely we have to play the part all the time,' he coaxed and she rolled her eyes. He had an answer for everything. Thank goodness they were back at the house and they could go their separate ways.

As luck would have it, they met Paul coming out just as they entered. He looked from one to the other, and Jack's strategically placed arm, and a big grin split his face.

'Hi, Jack. Ellie. Great to see you two have finally stopped fighting. Must be catching, this love stuff!' Laughing heartily, he jogged off to where he had parked his Land Rover.

Ellie watched him go, appalled. 'Oh, great! Now look what you've done!' she exclaimed, turning accusing eyes on Jack, who looked highly amused.

'Me?' he gasped, placing a hand on his chest and trying to look aggrieved.

'You had to play the fool, and now Paul's got entirely the wrong impression!'

Jack took her by the shoulders and gave her a tiny shake. 'You're making a mountain out of a molehill, Ellie. He was joking with us.'

Ellie set her jaw. 'Well, I didn't find it funny.'

'Do you want him to think you're still mooning over Luke, too?'

'Of course not. I just don't want him to think that we're involved now.'

Jack gave her an old-fashioned look. 'He won't have any option soon. The whole family is going to believe it. Get used to the idea.'

He was right, darn it, Ellie conceded with a grimace as she preceded him indoors and made for the stairs. They couldn't go about switching their supposed romance on and off. It had to be on all the time. She understood the sense of it, but it didn't make her feel any less jittery. Tell herself though she might that it was all a sham, somehow she couldn't quite get convinced.

She might just have jumped from the frying-pan to the fire after all.

CHAPTER FIVE

THAT very evening Jack dropped the bombshell on the family—Ellie included. She had had no inkling of what he intended to do. They had gone into town as planned but by early afternoon hadn't encountered Luke and Andrea, though Ellie did manage to find an engagement gift for them. So it wasn't a total waste of time. Jack had been in a relaxed mood and they had actually spent the time quite happily searching the markets, stopping off at a small local restaurant for some lunch when energy levels began to flag.

They ate outside, watching the world go by.

'So, how are things in the investment banking business? Still making disgusting amounts of money?' she teased him over coffee.

'You might say we're living in interesting times,' Jack returned ironically.

Her brows rose at the description. 'You didn't buy into those technology thingummys did you?' she asked, shaking her head and tut-tutting reprovingly.

His smile widened. 'Not as heavily as some,' he admitted, not in the least fazed by her teasing.

'So there's no chance of you being out of a job?'

'You can sleep safely in your bed at night, secure in the knowledge that I will still be able to support you in the style you've become accustomed to,' Jack returned smoothly.

'Hey!' Ellie objected instantly. 'You won't support

me in any style, I make my own living.' Worked hard at it too.

'Sure you do, but I keep my eye on your trust fund.'

That was different. The fund he was referring to was the one she had inherited from her grandmother. She had come into it when she was twenty-one, but she had never touched it, preferring to make her own way in life. 'Oh, that. How's it doing? Should I still trust you with it?'

Another man might have taken offence, but Jack merely looked amused at her doubting his financial acumen. 'It's doing well. If you bothered to check you'd find it had increased quite considerably. However, if you think someone else could do better...'

Ellie wasn't really worried about the money, and knew of nobody else who would look after her interests so well. 'On consideration I'll stick with you,' she conceded grudgingly and he grinned at her.

'Big of you.'

'Well,' Ellie grinned back. 'I know that when it comes to money you're totally trustworthy.'

One brow curved up. 'Meaning I'm not trustworthy in other ways? I think you should elaborate.' Reaching across the small table he began toying with her fingers. 'In what ways don't you trust me, Angel?' he went on huskily, and Ellie suddenly found herself caught on the end of a gaze simply loaded with sensual mockery.

She drew her hand back but not without a shiver of awareness. 'I wish you would stop doing that,' she complained, though the quaver in her voice rather spoiled the effect.

'Just getting into the mood,' he taunted and she rolled her eyes.

'That's just my point. There is no mood to get into.

You don't have to touch me but you do. I can't trust you not to take advantage of the situation.'

Jack laughed unrepentantly. 'Angel, if you felt nothing, it wouldn't matter if I touched you or not. Your problem is you don't trust yourself. I'm the least of your worries. What are you going to do when you don't want to say no any longer?'

She had been wondering that herself but, as she had no answer, her chin rose a notch. 'What makes you think that will happen?'

He sat forward, closing the gap between them. 'Because you and I are a combustible combination. No matter how hard you tamp down the flames, they keep coming back.'

Which was true enough, but she wasn't about to say so. 'I'm a pretty good fire fighter. I'll cope.'

His smile took on that sexy curl which weakened her knees, so it was as well she was sitting down. 'Sometimes you have to set a fire to control another. Maybe we should get together and check it out,' Jack suggested silkily and Ellie uttered a groaning laugh.

'You have an answer for everything.'

'Not everything, Angel, or you and I would be somewhere a lot less public, doing something much more interesting than searching for my brother.'

Ellie shook her head, though her nerves did a high jump at his statement. 'There you go again, assuming I'd agree to be somewhere else with you. What an ego!'

Smiling, Jack rose smoothly to his feet and reached into his pocket for money to pay their bill. 'One day you're going to start being honest with yourself, and I intend to be around when you do. Come on, let's take another tour of the shops. In a town the size of this one, they have to be somewhere close.'

'I am being honest. It's you who has a lack of faith,' Ellie protested as she joined him. 'You don't believe anything I say.'

He laughed softly. 'That's because your lips say one thing and the rest of you another. You'll be incredible when you finally come to terms with yourself,' he told her, taking her hand in his and resisting all her attempts to pull away.

'Let me go,' she hissed through her teeth, very much aware that her undignified struggles were drawing a great deal of attention to herself, and not liking it.

'Behave yourself then,' he commanded continuing on his way to where the shops sold all sorts of things for the tourist trade. 'Be a good girl and I'll buy you a present.'

Abandoning her fruitless bid for freedom with a glare at his back, Ellie followed along like a grumpy dog on a leash, though in actual fact the way his hand held hers so securely, she was experiencing that strange bubbly feeling inside again.

'I don't want you to buy me a present,' she pouted.

'Tough,' came the short response. 'Ah, here we are.' He stopped at a display but didn't release her.

Glowering at his back, she poked her tongue out. 'I hate you.'

Jack shot her a grin over his shoulder. 'No you don't. You only think you do. Now, if I let you go, do you promise to behave and not run off.'

Ellie smiled at him sweetly. 'I'm going to hit you in a minute, Jack,' she threatened, but all he did was laugh—though he did finally release her.

All at once her hand felt strangely lost. It was amazing how such a simple touch had made her feel secure.

Which was sheer lunacy. She was going crazy. There was no other reason for it. Stark, staring…

'There you are,' Jack declared with satisfaction, plopping a hat down on her head. 'Now you can get rid of the other one.'

'You bought me a hat?' she exclaimed in surprise.

'I thought it was about time you had a new one.'

Automatically Ellie reached up and took it off to examine it. It was large and floppy, and the colour of sunflowers. You'd never lose me in a crowd, she thought wryly, and knew that she loved it. For no good reason her throat closed over.

'Thank you, it's lovely,' she said gruffly replacing it and setting it at a jaunty angle.

'You're welcome,' Jack responded softly and, when he took her hand again, she made no protest.

As luck would have it, they finally bumped into Luke and Andrea when they had decided to give the search up as a bad job and return to the villa. The couple were standing outside a boutique and appeared to be arguing.

'All does not seem to be well with the happy couple,' Ellie observed drily, vastly amused by the badgered expression on Luke's face.

'Hmm,' Jack agreed. 'There does seem to be a frosty nip to the air over there. Let's go see what's wrong.'

Jack hailed them as they strolled closer, and it was almost comical the way Luke and Andrea stopped fighting and plastered smiles on their faces. 'Hi there,' Jack greeted them when they met up. 'It looked like you could use a referee.'

Andrea immediately slipped her arm through Luke's and waved a dismissive hand. 'It was nothing.'

'A lovers' tiff? You should kiss and make up,' Ellie suggested jauntily, and the other woman smiled tightly.

'Not in public. I leave that kind of display to those less particular,' she shuddered delicately, and Ellie was left in no doubt Andrea was referring to the kiss she and Jack had shared last night.

Jack recognised it too, and laughed at her. 'You should try unbending a bit, Andrea, it can be fun.'

Andrea stiffened at the inference that she was too up-tight, and sensing his fiancée's mood Luke cut in quickly. 'What brings you here?'

'Shopping,' Jack obligingly changed tack. 'I wanted to buy Ellie a new hat. The old one was long past its sell-by date,' he enlarged.

'Didn't I give you that hat?' Luke queried, eyes narrowing.

'That's right,' Ellie affirmed, staring him out. 'I thought it was great when I was fifteen, but it's dated now. This one is fantastic. I just love the colour,' she added brightly. 'What do you think Andrea?'

'It's a little garish for my taste, but it suits you, Ellie,' Andrea returned, and Ellie couldn't be certain whether she was being told yellow suited her, or she was a garish person. She rather thought it would be the latter.

'Oh, well, each to their own!' she said cheerfully, not about to be offended by an opinion that didn't matter to her. 'Are you going back to the villa now?'

'Not yet. There are a few shops Andrea hasn't been in yet,' Luke joked and got a frosty look for his pains.

'OK, we'll see you both at dinner, then,' Jack replied and, taking Ellie's hand once more, they turned away from the other couple and headed for where they had left the car. Ellie could feel two pairs of eyes on her back for a long time until the crowd swallowed them up.

'Andrea doesn't seem to like you,' Jack observed mockingly when they were safely out of earshot.

Ellie grinned up at him. 'I know. It's shattering.'

'So I see,' he grinned back.

'Isn't she awful!' Ellie exclaimed with a grimace. 'Can you imagine being married to her?'

Jack shuddered. 'I can, and I'm glad the lady is spoken for. I suppose I ought to feel sorry for Luke, but somehow I feel he's getting what he deserves.'

'I am so glad you're nothing like him,' Ellie went on earnestly, and he looked amused.

'I'm glad you're glad,' he responded and, as he smiled down into her eyes, Ellie experienced the strangest sensation. Something powerful passed between them. It was as if a bond had been forged, but quite what it meant she wasn't sure. All she did know was that it wasn't alarming. Far from it. She felt at ease with him, and it made her frown.

'Something wrong?' he asked, but Ellie shook her head.

'Not exactly. It's just…you're different from what I remember.'

One eyebrow quirked. 'I'm still me, but maybe you see me differently because you're different yourself. Have you thought of that?'

She hadn't, but she knew she had changed a lot these past six months, so he was probably right. 'Maybe,' she agreed.

Jack released her hand only to slip his arm about her shoulders. 'Don't worry about it. The past is another country. If we're wise, we won't go back there. You have to look ahead, see what you want and go for it.'

'Is that what you're doing?' she asked curiously.

'All the time, Angel. All the time. Come on, let's go

home. I could do with a shower and something cool to drink.'

Ellie didn't argue, for the prospect sounded wonderful. It had become stiflingly hot, and a shower sounded like bliss. Then, because she was still feeling the effect of the travelling from the day before, she intended to collapse onto her bed and sleep. And if she should dream about a certain person, she wouldn't be at all surprised.

There was a full house for dinner that evening and, as ever when the whole family was present, it was a lively occasion, with everyone having something to say and trying to say it louder than the rest. The family didn't gather together very often, which was why a tradition of meeting in the summer had grown over time. Everyone had to be brought up to date with what was happening, and it generally took the entire length of the meal to do it.

Afterwards, they all drifted out onto the terrace to drink coffee and soak up the scents and atmosphere of Capri. It was no wonder to Ellie that the Roman Emperors had chosen to have villas here, for it was perfect for relaxing and forgetting the stresses of everyday life. As the moon rose, she sighed in contentment. No matter where she went in the world, this place would always have a home in her heart.

'I've arranged a small party for you and Andrea, Luke,' Mary Thornton told her stepson some time later, when there was a brief lull in the conversation.

'You didn't have to do that, Mrs Thornton,' Andrea responded, before Luke could say a word, sounding just a tad aghast at the prospect to Ellie's sensitive ears. She had been quick to notice a coolness on the other woman's part to the other members of the family. It was as if they didn't quite meet her criteria for people to know, and Ellie found that offensive.

'Come now, you must call me Mary. Mrs Thornton is far too formal for us. And of course I had to do something. If you're to be married in America, then none of our friends will be able to attend the service. There are many people who've known Luke since he was small, and they will want to wish him well, so this is the best way all round,' Mary declared, smiling encouragingly at Luke's fiancée.

'I expect Andrea was just thinking of the amount of work it would be, Mary,' Jack put in casually, but the glance he shot his prospective sister-in-law spoke volumes, she would upset his stepmother at her peril.

Andrea tensed at the silent rebuke but wisely took the hint. 'Of course that's what I meant... Mary. Luke and I never expected you to go to so much trouble just for us,' she said with a tiny laugh.

'Don't worry, we'll all pitch in and help. Paul's a dab hand at putting things on sticks if you can drag him away from his computer,' Ellie put in teasingly, and he threatened to throw his coffee over her.

Everyone else laughed, but Andrea's chin visibly dropped. 'Things on sticks? You won't be using a caterer?'

Mary chose not to hear the dismay in her voice. 'Our housekeeper is a wonderful cook, and we enjoy doing the catering ourselves. It's half the fun. Not that I expect you to do anything, Andrea. You and Luke are the guests of honour, so you'll be allowed to make yourselves scarce.'

The relief on the pair of faces almost made Ellie laugh out loud. An imp of devilment took control and she composed her features into a serious look. 'Of course, those who don't help out front are left with the washing-up, but that's only fair,' she said solemnly, and had to bite down hard on her lip when Andrea paled. Then voices spoke up.

'Oh, Ellie!' her mother exclaimed with a laugh.

'Don't listen to her, darling, she's having you on!' Luke advised, shooting his stepsister a poisonous look.

Tom Thornton took pity on his soon to be daughter-in-law. 'You'll get used to Ellie's sense of humour, Andrea. Don't worry, we have a machine to do the washing, as she very well knows. Would you like me to freshen up your coffee, or would you prefer something stronger?'

Ellie watched as her stepfather went off to get the chardonnay Andrea had requested, and jumped when a hand closed on her thigh. She glanced round into a pair of dancing blue eyes.

'Take it easy,' Jack advised softly from his seat on the lounger next to hers.

'If she looks down her nose at my mother again, I might forget I'm a lady,' Ellie returned heatedly. Her mother was the friendliest of souls, and didn't deserve to have Andrea acting as if she had the plague.

'Mary knows how to deal with people like dear Andrea. Leave it to her to fight her own battle. You might be surprised.'

Ellie looked to where her mother was talking to the other woman and not looking in the least disturbed. 'You think she might sock her?' she asked hopefully, but Jack laughed.

'Her methods are far more subtle. Andrea will be given just so much rope, then Mary will utter a few quiet words and I'll guarantee that dear Andrea will be put well and truly in her place. So you can pull in your claws, tiger.'

Ellie sank back into her seat and sent him a knowing look. 'In which case you can take your hand off my thigh now,' she commanded him drily.

'Spoilsport,' he grumbled, but complied. Then made her jump again when he took her hand, lacing his fingers through hers.

'What are you doing?' she queried, and promptly gasped when he raised her hand to his lips and kissed the back of it. Heads turned, and Ellie laughed nervously as colour rose in her cheeks. 'Jack, cut it out!'

Instead of doing so he brought his lips close to her ear in what would look like a highly intimate moment between lovers. 'Too late for that. Just go with the flow, Angel,' he advised in a whisper that sent shivers down her spine.

Glancing round, Ellie saw her mother and stepfather exchange glances and could have died. Before she could do or say anything, though, Jack had risen to his feet and was pulling her to hers.

'Ellie and I are just going to take a little moonlight stroll. We may be some time,' he explained and she found herself being whisked away to the steps which led to the garden.

Ellie didn't know whether to laugh or stamp her foot at the way he had dropped this particular bombshell. Everyone would know they were an item now.

'Wow, that was subtle!' she exclaimed when there was little chance of them being overheard. 'You could have let me know what you intended to do!'

'I could have,' Jack replied, steering her down a path. 'But I didn't think your acting ability would be up to it.'

'You know what they're all going to think, don't you?' she grumbled.

'Naturally. They think we want to do some furtive fumbling in the dark,' Jack retorted, and she could tell from the tremor in his voice that he was finding the situation hilarious.

By contrast she felt murderous. 'I'll never be able to look my mother in the eye again.'

'Of course you will,' Jack pooh-poohed that. 'She was young once, too, you know.'

She shot a dagger look into his back. 'I didn't come down in the last shower of rain you know. So you'd better understand that there won't be any furtive fumbling going on,' she warned, then almost bumped into him when he stopped. Her chin went up and she dared him to do anything.

'Stop being a pain, Eleanora, and relax. I'm not about to do anything furtive,' Jack conceded, but she barely had time to feel a fleeting moment of relief before her pulled the rug out from under her. 'When I kiss you, it's going to be in full view of anyone watching.'

She was speechless, and he took advantage of it to slip his arm about her waist and urge her unresisting form along the path that bounded the hillside. A wall had been built to prevent accidents, and it was against this that he chose to lean, pulling her into the vee of his legs. His hands dropped to span her hips and Ellie knew that she couldn't pull away in case they were being observed.

'Still mad?' Jack asked, eyes twinkling in the moonlight, and the part of her that wasn't angry found them fascinating.

'By rights I ought to push you right over the edge,' she grumbled, knowing she was trapped.

'But you won't,' he said with such utter assurance she was instantly irritated.

'How can you be so sure?' she demanded and a slow smile spread across his lips.

'Because you want me to kiss you as much as I do,' he pronounced huskily and, if it hadn't been true before, it was certainly true now.

Being this close to him was pure temptation. She couldn't help but recall the kisses they had shared—and how they had made her feel. She had done her best to ignore it all day, but now, here with him like this, so close it would take little more than a breath to bring them together, she had to admit she wanted him to kiss her again. No, not merely wanted, needed.

'You're taking an unfair advantage because you know I can't fight you here. You've got a nerve!'

That brought a quirky grin to his lips and a sultry glow to his eyes. 'More than one, and they're all registering off the scale,' he growled sexily, and her own nerves began rippling like crazy.

Still she fought it. 'Stop flirting with me. I'm not going to let you get away with this. And I'm not going to kiss you!' she exclaimed, planting her hands firmly on his shoulders to keep the necessary distance between them.

He nodded past her. 'What, and dash everyone's expectations? They're all just waiting for the main event to start.'

Ellie had to curb the temptation to turn and find out for herself if they were being watched. Jack could be lying but, knowing her family, she knew that they would more than likely have an audience. Which was exactly what Jack had relied upon. He had manufactured the situation to put their relationship squarely on the map—as she had agreed—and she was caught.

'So,' he urged softly. 'What's it to be?'

Ellie licked her lips nervously, and felt her nerves jolt when his eyes followed the movement. 'I think I've made a pact with the devil,' she retorted gruffly.

'Why, because I'm tempting you?' Jack teased huskily.

Oh, he was tempting her all right. Her hands could feel the firmness of his shoulders and the heat of his body. His scent was an intoxication, and the press of his thighs on hers was setting her stomach quivering. She was fighting herself as much as him to keep the distance between them, because inside she just wanted to press closer and drown in his kiss as she had before. Her eyes dropped to his mouth, and it was a fatal error, because it only served to remind her of the magic it could create.

'Damn. Damn. Damn,' she whispered in a choked voice. 'I should be stronger than this,' she berated herself, even as her hands began to glide around his neck. 'What do you do to me?'

'Only what you do to me. Now, put us both out of our misery and kiss me,' he ordered tautly.

It was that desperate tone in his voice which did for her. The need it conveyed struck a chord deep within her, and she just had to kiss him. The distance closed and her lips touched his. The heat of them made her give a tiny gasp as his mouth opened over hers, then his tongue sought entry and all thought vanished. Passion caught fire at each stroke, reaching flash point in seconds.

Ellie moaned low in her throat as the throbbing ache of desire grew inside her. Just like that she wanted him and, from the hardness of his body, she was left in no doubt that he wanted her just as powerfully. She had never wanted anyone like this. Had never had her passions aroused to swiftly, nor ached so painfully for another human being. It was overwhelming and, in danger of losing all reason, she dragged her mouth away, drawing in deep gulps of air.

'Enough!' she cried in little more than a broken whisper.

Jack watched her from eyes blazing with barely contained passion. 'Hell, Angel, kissing is never going to be enough. You know it as well as I do. Stop fighting it, Ellie.'

'I have to,' she argued shakily.

'Why?'

Ellie groaned, resting her forehead on his. 'Because I don't want to want you, damn it.'

'What do you want me to do about it?' he asked wryly and she sighed because she knew there was nothing he could do.

'You don't happen to have a magic lamp tucked away somewhere, do you?'

Jack swore softly. 'Damn, I knew there was something I meant to pack!'

She laughed tiredly. 'Very funny.'

Reaching up, Jack framed her face with his hands and eased her away so he could see her. 'You're worrying too much.'

She frowned. 'Why aren't you worrying at all? Doesn't it bother you—the speed of this thing? I mean, why you? Why me? Why now?'

'Damned if I know. I only know this is a pretty powerful attraction, and I'm not about to walk away from it,' Jack answered simply.

Ellie swallowed to moisten a dry throat. 'What if it turns out to be a mistake?'

'Then we learn from it,' he said reasonably. 'Just understand this, Angel. It isn't going to go away. Something this powerful doesn't evaporate overnight. If you don't deal with it now, you'll only have to deal with it later.'

She knew he spoke nothing less than the truth, but it didn't make her feel any happier. This had all been too much, and she needed to be alone to think.

'Have we given them enough of a show for one night? Can we go now?'

'I should imagine the message has got across. But are you sure you don't want to sample a little more of the moonlight?' he teased her and, despite her worries, she laughed.

'I think I've experienced enough moon madness for one night. Heaven only knows what Mum and Dad are going to make of this.'

Jack eased her away as he stood up, and Ellie shivered slightly at the disappearance of his warmth. 'Take my word for it, they won't even mention it. This is between us.'

Ellie hoped he was right, for she didn't know what she would say if her mother did decide to ask questions. What she did know for certain was that there was no way out now. The relationship between herself and Jack had been established and they could only perpetuate it. The need for it hadn't changed, but it no longer seemed the bigger problem.

All Luke had to do was believe the relationship was real and she would be free of him. What troubled her was now just how real the relationship was becoming.

CHAPTER SIX

SHAM or not, a week later, it was clear to Ellie that the strategy was paying off. In the beginning they had had to take some ribbing about the turn of events, but, much to her surprise, in no time at all, she and Jack were an accepted couple. Nobody appeared to think it the least odd that they should have been at loggerheads one moment and supposedly inseparable the next. Nobody except Luke, that was. Though he was careful not to show it, her experience of him told her he was not impressed.

As each day passed, and he watched her with Jack, his mood grew angrier. At first Ellie couldn't resist checking for signs that the message was getting through, but increasingly she found herself forgetting about him altogether. Her concentration had quickly become centred solely on Jack. She had expected to be uncomfortable with her role, but that was proving far from the truth. As she had suspected it would, the line between reality and pretence had begun to blur.

Mainly because the attraction between them, always strong, was growing. It was there all the time, unspoken but oh so powerful. It wasn't long before Ellie discovered that the more she was with him, the more she wanted to be with him. So far she had been able to keep him at bay, but it was becoming harder. When he kissed her, and he did so often, she was finding it difficult to remember this was just an act. Somehow she had always managed to stop before things got too out of hand, but her defences were extremely shaky. Jack never complained or tried to take things further, but accepted her no—when she managed to say it. No matter how far things had gone, he was always self-controlled.

When she found herself wishing he would lose that impressive control for once, and override her objections, she knew she was in trouble. Her resistance had vanished somewhere along the line. Being honest with herself, she knew she no longer wanted to fight the attraction. All she really wanted to do was give in to it and let it take her where it would. It was only pride which kept her battling. Jack was certain she would surrender—so of course she couldn't.

She had been musing on her ability to keep doing that last night when Luke had sought her out in the laundry room, where she had been sorting out some washing. Absorbed in her thoughts, she hadn't heard him enter, and nearly jumped out of her skin when she turned and discovered him standing there. She almost dropped the basket of clean clothes, and hastily retrieved it before anything fell out onto the floor.

'Oh, God, you gave me a fright!' she exclaimed, pressing a hand to her racing heart.

'What's going on, Ellie?' Luke demanded curtly and, though she knew what he meant, she chose to misunderstand him.

'I'm sorting the washing. There are some things I want for tomorrow,' she explained obligingly, and was secretly pleased to see flags of colour in his cheeks.

'I meant what's going on with you and my brother?' he ground out tersely, and it did her morale a power of good to know she was getting to him at last.

'Come on, Luke. I'm sure I don't need to draw you

a picture,' she goaded him, turning back to the tumble-dryer. Setting the basket on top, she began putting the clothes in.

Luke caught her arm in an uncomfortably tight grip and tugged her round to face him. 'I see it, but I don't believe it. You've never wanted Jack. It was me you wanted.'

Ellie tried to prise his hand away but he merely tightened his grip. Hiding a wince, she smiled at him coldly. 'Did. Past tense. I don't want you now. I think I've made that more than clear.'

Luke's mouth twisted nastily. 'Using him against me isn't going to work. He's a pitiful substitute for me. Did you know he fell in love years ago with a mystery woman and still carries a torch for her. What a chump.'

To hear Luke talk so disparagingly of his brother made Ellie go cold with anger. He had no right to speak of Jack that way. No right at all. 'Jack's more of a man than you'll ever be!' she waded in with an explosion of fury. 'At least it proves he has a heart. Something you will never have. Jack will never be a substitute for anyone! He's the genuine article. Now let...me...go!' she gritted out and finally managed to break free of his iron grasp.

Clearly Luke didn't care for her opinion. 'I'd be careful what I said, if I were you.'

Ellie glared at him glacially. 'Is that a threat? Then here's one for you. Don't ever let me hear you talking about Jack like that again.'

Luke laughed, and it was an unpleasant sound. 'My God, he must be good in bed if he's got you defending him like a tigress with her young!'

He was so way off the mark it was laughable, but

Ellie wasn't laughing. 'What goes on between Jack and me is none of your business.'

Luke's eyes narrowed. 'I could make it my business. What do you think he would say if he knew about us?'

'What do you think Andrea would say if she knew you wanted to have her and me, and you not even married?' Ellie shot right back, and that had Luke backing off in a hurry.

'You won't say anything to her, do you hear me?' he ordered, jabbing a finger at her to emphasise the point.

Ellie stared him out. 'I hear you. Now you hear me. Leave Jack alone.'

This time Luke laughed aloud. 'My God, and you used to think of him as the devil incarnate.'

She smiled. 'I used to think you were wonderful, but I haven't thought that way for a very long time now.'

Luke's expression turned thoughtful. 'Are you in love with him?' he asked, and for some reason that made her heart lurch wildly. Yet she kept her expression stony.

'Won't Andrea be wondering where you are?'

To her relief he took the hint, but turned at the door. 'This isn't over,' he warned, and went out.

Ellie let out a ragged breath and sank back against the dryer. She was shaking, but it wasn't from fear. It was anger. His disparaging comments about Jack had stirred up a veritable hornets' nest inside her and she was still buzzing. She should have punched him on the nose when she had the chance, she thought. He deserved it, and more.

She began stuffing clothes into the dryer with more force than they deserved, and it wasn't until some time had passed that a thought struck her. *Why* was she so angry on Jack's behalf? He meant nothing to her. OK, so she was attracted, but that was purely physical. Yet she had flown to his defence like a wild thing.

It was probably because she hated injustice, she told herself, and Luke's remarks had been unjust. Her nerves stopped jangling. Yes, that had to be it. It wasn't right that Luke, a man with little integrity, should mock a man who had it in spades.

The rationalisation made her feel more comfortable with herself, and she finished off the washing in a more settled frame of mind.

That had been yesterday. Today, the four of them were on the beach. It had been Jack's suggestion that they make up a party, and he had hired a motor boat to take them to a secluded spot on a nearby island. Ellie had agreed, though she thought he was crazy. The idea of spending a whole day with the 'happy couple' had made her shudder. She and Andrea did not get along any better now than in the beginning. They were polite to each other, but nothing more—for it had been made clear to Ellie that she fell a long way short of Andrea's high standards. A fact she was inordinately grateful for, as it kept them apart for most of the time.

She wondered if Andrea's high standards would cause her to ignore Luke's infidelities—of which Ellie had no doubt there would be many, for Luke would not change. Had it been any other woman, she would have pitied her finding out, but Andrea was welcome to all that was coming.

'Penny for them,' Jack offered from beside her, and she glanced down to where he lay stretched out on the picnic blanket they shared.

She had avoided looking at him ever since they got here for, like her, he was dressed in skimpy swimming gear. His bronzed body had proved as tantalising as she remembered, and she had carefully kept her gaze averted. It hadn't stopped her from being vitally aware of him though, and the only way she had been able to resist the urge to touch him was to look anywhere but at him. From the glint in his eye now, he knew exactly what she was doing—and more importantly, why.

'I was just wondering if Andrea really knows what she's doing,' she said truthfully.

Jack came up on one elbow and followed Ellie's gaze to where Luke swam whilst Andrea hovered uncomfortably at the water's edge. 'I think she does. She wants him, warts and all.'

Ellie brought her knees up and wrapped her arms around them. 'How can she want him? He's never been faithful to anyone in his life.' She knew that from personal experience.

'You tell me,' Jack drawled mockingly. 'You wanted him yourself not so very long ago.'

She felt warmth flood her cheeks. 'Thank you for reminding me I showed distinct lack of judgement in my choice of men,' she responded wryly. 'But, like I told you the other day, I'm well and truly over him now,' she added, turning to look at Jack to make sure he believed her. She didn't want there to be any doubt.

Jack searched her eyes for an age before he nodded and lay back down again. 'Speaking as his brother, I never could see what you saw in him anyway,' he taunted softly, and she laughed—mostly at herself.

'Oh, Luke cuts a very romantic figure. He's handsome and dashing. A free spirit who loves to break the rules. A girl gets caught up in the romance of it all, but it's all show and no substance.'

'Something I tried to tell you more than once,' Jack returned drily, and she pulled a face at him.

'What teenager wants to listen to the voice of reason? We're all in love with the idea of being in love. Being sensible isn't on the agenda.'

'So had I left you alone, you would have seen the light sooner?' he charged her and her lips twisted into a wry smile.

'Probably not. At the time I was wrapped up it would have taken something more powerful to knock some sense into me,' she admitted.

'And what monumental act caused your vision to clear?'

Ellie knew she couldn't reveal the truth, but she kept as close to it as she was able. 'Actually, I saw him in London when he spent some time there. He was never with the same woman twice, and I looked at him and realised he wasn't the man I always thought he was. The scales fell away, and I knew I'd been in love with love, not Luke at all.'

Jack frowned. 'Luke never mentioned seeing you.'

Her nerves fluttered as she wondered if she had said too much, but she stared him out. 'Come on, Jack. You know Luke only tells people what he wants them to know. He's like an iceberg. Four-fifths of him are under water.'

He looked at her curiously. 'Suddenly you seem to know him very well.'

Ellie shrugged. To know him a little was to know him well when your eyes were open. 'I've known him a long time.'

'And for most of that time you were wearing blinkers.'

Ellie was rapidly beginning to wish she had never started the conversation. Without intending to she had aroused his curiosity, and that was the very last thing she wanted. 'I thought the idea was that I should see the light about Luke. Surely the swiftness of it is irrelevant?' she retorted irritably, and Jack sat up in one smooth movement.

'Believe me, it is. I guess it's hard to accept that I don't have to chafe you about him any longer.'

'Don't worry, you'll soon find something else to tease me about. *You* haven't changed,' she told him with a sardonic grin.

Jack smiled at her, and there was a sultry look in his eyes when he spoke. 'Trust me, Ellie. I can think of far more interesting things to do than tease you,' he promised and set her pulse quickening instantly.

Her mouth went dry, and she hastily licked her lips, very much aware that his eyes followed the action minutely. 'Is that so?' she challenged breathlessly.

'Uh-huh,' Jack confirmed, reaching out to run one finger gently along the curve of her arm.

Just like that the temperature on their particular part of the beach, rose quite significantly, making it difficult to breathe. Ellie was caught in the fire of his gaze like a moth, and to look into those blue depths was like drowning.

'This is crazy,' she whispered. 'You shouldn't be having this effect on me.' Not when she had sworn to steer clear of men, and this one in particular. But her instinct for self-preservation was fast disappearing. Saving herself wasn't even an option. All she wanted to do right then was plunge deeper.

His finger traced on down to her wrist, and she didn't

resist when he enfolded her wrist and tugged her hand free. 'What effect am I having?'

'You know,' she sighed, and Jack laughed softly.

'Be more specific,' he ordered, bending his head to kiss the tender skin of her wrist, then stopped abruptly. His head came up sharply. 'What's this?' he queried in a voice so far removed from seductive, it caused her to blink and look down.

There, a little way up her forearm, was a row of tiny bruises. The result of the force with which Luke had held her arm last night. Which, naturally, she could not tell him. 'It's nothing. I slipped in the bath and bumped it on the tap,' she invented. Rather neatly, she thought. Until Jack looked at her sceptically.

'A tap with four fingers and a thumb, apparently,' he jibed, and she flushed guiltily, which didn't help her cause at all.

'It's just a bruise, Jack,' she returned dismissively.

If she hoped to put him off, she was doomed to failure. His jaw became set and he held her gaze steadily. 'That's the size of a man's hand, and it must have hurt. Who did it, Ellie?'

'It wasn't intentional. I just bruise easily,' she rallied, trying to make light of it. 'Stop making such a fuss!'

'Being fussy is deciding which table napkins to put out. Someone wasn't gentle with you, and I want to know who it was,' Jack insisted doggedly.

'For what purpose?'

'So I can tell them in no uncertain terms, that they won't do it again. Nobody manhandles you and gets away with it.'

Ellie couldn't recall the last time anyone had come to her defence so insistently. Luke certainly never had. She stared at him in amazement, whilst a warm feeling began to swell in her chest. Irritating though it was to know he wouldn't let it go, it was incredibly heartening to discover he cared what happened to her.

She smiled at him, her expression half amazed, half amused. 'I didn't know you worried about me so much.'

'I told you there were a lot of things you didn't know about me,' he reminded her.

'You were right.'

Jack tipped his head to one side, observing her sardonically. 'You aren't going to tell me, are you?'

Ellie knew she wanted to but couldn't, and shook her head. 'No.'

He let out his breath in a long sigh. 'One day you're going to trust me enough to tell me the truth.'

Her gaze fell away, dropping to where he still cupped her wrist in his hand. Telling him the truth wasn't a matter of trust. The deception had gone on too long, and she and Luke had made fools of their family by that deception. They would be hurt by the truth, and she wouldn't blame them for being disappointed.

Looking at his hand, she realised again how different Jack was from what she had always believed. Having discovered that he didn't think so badly of her after all, she knew she didn't want to disappoint him now. In consequence, telling the truth was further out of the question. As for trusting him...

'I do trust you, Jack,' she said seriously, looking up, and knew as she said it that it was no less than the truth.

The confession brought a wry smile to his lips. 'With qualifications.'

She raised her shoulders helplessly. 'I'm sure there are things in your life you don't intend to tell anyone, and trust has nothing to do with the decision,' she pointed out reasonably, and he groaned.

'As always, you're right. So I'll say no more about the bruises—on one condition. If whoever did it bothers you again, you'll tell me. I don't intend to stand by and watch you get hurt if there's something I can do to prevent it,' Jack pronounced stoutly, and she couldn't help but smile.

'I never saw you as a white knight before. It suits you,' she teased, but Jack was not about to be diverted.

'Your word, Ellie, or I'll nag you ragged,' he threatened, and Ellie knew it was no empty threat.

'OK, I give you my word, but nothing is going to happen. I told you it was unintentional.'

Jack snorted in disbelief. 'If holding you that tight was the only way to save your life, that's unintentional. Anything else is deliberate. Most men are stronger than women. Not inflicting damage when harm can so easily be done, is something a man prides himself on.'

Ellie found her throat closing over as he spoke, for there was a nobility to Jack that she had been so ignorant of and, by that ignorance, she felt that she had somehow failed him. It was the weirdest feeling, and she had no idea where it came from or what it meant. She just knew she had to respond to it.

'She missed out on something special,' she declared with an edge of wistfulness, and Jack frowned.

'Who did?'

'The woman you're in love with.' He blinked, and she realised her line of thought had clearly taken him by surprise. 'I know you probably don't want to talk about it, but I just want to say, had things turned out differently, I know she would have been proud to be married to you.'

The oddest expression crossed his face, but it vanished in a flash and in the next second he was on his feet, pulling her up with him.

'You're right, I don't want to talk about it. Let's go for a swim instead,' he suggested, and without waiting for her to agree, he headed off down the beach, tugging her along behind him.

That he still cared deeply for the unknown woman, was made clear to her by his reaction, and she was caught by a stab of envy. Before she knew better, she had hoped that Luke would love her like that, but he didn't possess the capability to love selflessly. She, on the other hand, had a lot of love to give to the right man—if she was ever ready to risk her heart again.

Jack released her hand as they ran into the water, and she couldn't help smiling as she watched him dive into the next wave and disappear from view. He had always been at home in the water, and looked as if he still swam often from the tone of his muscles. Wading further in, she glanced around expectantly, waiting for him to pop up again, but the seconds passed and his dark head failed to appear.

A dart of alarm speared through her. Where was he? She knew Jack was a strong swimmer, but surely even he couldn't stay under water this long. She spun round, eyes furiously searching for sign of him, but he was nowhere to be seen. Her heart started to pound anxiously as she thought of all the possibilities. He could have got caught in something and be unable to surface!

'Jack!' Ellie called as she waded further out, though it was doubtful that he would have heard her.

Telling herself not to panic, because that wouldn't help him, she was just about to call again, when she felt herself being grabbed by the ankles and in the next instant her feet were being pulled out from under her. Ellie just had time to take in a gasp of air before she disappeared under the surface. She bobbed up again, coughing and spluttering, just as an arm came around her from behind and she was eased backwards onto the safety of a strong male body.

'I've got you. You're safe now,' Jack's laughing voice declared next to her right ear and, had she not been floating and had a hand free, she would have boxed his ears for the scare he had put her through.

'That wasn't funny, Jack!' she exclaimed angrily, and ground her teeth when he had the nerve to laugh. 'I was safe before!'

'Mmm, but you're safer here in my arms, where I can keep an eye on you,' he countered seductively, sending those inevitable tiny shivers through her system.

She wanted to stay angry, but his body was moving rhythmically beneath her as he kept them afloat, and it was creating a warmth all of its own. Ellie could feel herself softening, which wasn't at all what she wanted to be feeling—alluring as it was. She was angry with him, and intended to stay that way. He couldn't be allowed to charm her out of it that easily.

'Don't you dare try to seduce me! I'm furious with you, Jack. I thought you'd drowned, for heaven's sake!' she protested, struggling to be free of him. But he refused to release her.

'Would you have missed me if I had?' he taunted softly, and she just knew he was smiling.

Deflating him was paramount. 'Of course I would

have. I don't have that big a family that I can afford to lose a member!' she retorted smartly.

'But I'm not really family, am I? I mean, there's no blood tie between us.'

'Maybe not,' Ellie agreed as they lazily rode the swell, 'but I've always thought of you as a brother.'

'Ah, but right now your thoughts are no more sisterly than mine are brotherly.'

'Speak for yourself,' she advised, though it was all too lamentably true. Once more she tried to break away from him, and this time succeeded. Expecting to touch bottom, she didn't realise Jack had towed them further out. Almost going under, she was forced to make a grab for his shoulders to keep herself afloat. Treading water, she glared at him. 'You could at least have warned me I was out of my depth!'

'You're not out of your depth, Ellie, you're just finding your feet,' Jack responded silkily, and the gleam in his eye left her in little doubt that they weren't talking about swimming. 'Besides, I would never let you drown alone. It's much more fun together.'

Ellie closed her eyes helplessly as his charm wound invisible threads about her. There was something to that saying *soft words turneth away wrath*. How could she be angry with him when he said things like that! Sighing ruefully, she shook her head. 'You're incorrigible.'

Jack tutted. 'No, you've got that wrong, Angel. I'm encouragable. Extremely encouragable. In fact, right now you're encouraging me to do this…'

Before Ellie had a chance to anticipate what he was going to do, he had framed her head with his hands, and brought his mouth down on hers. Then his legs wrapped themselves around hers and they slid under the water.

The absence of sight and sound made the sense of touch all the greater. Ellie forgot about everything except the pleasure of returning the kiss. Letting her tongue engage in an erotic dance with his that heated up the blood and rekindled that ache of longing deep within her. Every throb of her pulse was a clamour for more.

Then it was over. Far too soon for her enthralled senses. Lost as she was, she wasn't aware that she needed air until a powerful thrust of Jack's legs brought them shooting to the surface, and she was able to take a deep gasping lungful of oxygen. Breathing hard and wiping the water from her eyes she was pleased to see Jack was taking deep breaths too, which meant he had been as caught up as she.

'How do you do it?' he asked as they trod water again.

Ellie licked lips bruised by the passion of his kiss. 'How do I do what?'

'Make me lose all sense of self-preservation. Drowning wasn't supposed to be on the agenda today. You're a dangerous woman,' he accused her, but there was a light in his eyes that set her errant nerves skipping.

Though a tiny part of her brain advised caution, she ignored it. 'Does this mean you aren't going to kiss me again?' she flirted with a tiny smile curving the corners of her mouth. His eyes followed it and it was as if she had been touched by flame.

'Hell, no. I'll just have to remember to keep my feet firmly on the ground in future.'

'But I thought you wanted to be swept away.'

'Swept away, yes. Drowned, no. Not unless it's in a sea of passion with you. The Mediterranean is fine for swimming, but for drowning you need a bed. Anywhere—with you in it,' he came back, turning her blood to liquid fire, and setting her stomach clenching with desire.

He was turning her on so fast, she felt more than a little dizzy. 'I think I need to get back to shore,' she said in a husky voice. 'Right now.'

'You're right,' Jack agreed. 'This isn't the time or place.'

It wasn't what she meant at all, but anything that got her away from temptation and back to the safety of the shore was acceptable. They swam back, Jack matching his stroke to hers so that they arrived together. There he surprised her yet again by sweeping her up into his arms as he strode up the beach to the blanket.

'I can walk,' Ellie protested, even as she slipped her arms about his neck.

'I know, Angel, but we're being watched. Smile and wave like a good girl now,' he directed sardonically.

Glancing round, she found they were indeed the centre of attention of the couple already seated on the blanket. Obediently she smiled and waved. Andrea raised a limp hand, but Luke remained impassive.

When Jack lowered her to the blanket, Ellie batted her eyelashes at him provocatively. 'My hero!' she gasped, grinning, and he made to swat her with the towel he'd begun running over his hair.

'You've put on weight since the last time I carried you,' Jack complained dropping down beside her and finger-combing his hair into order, leaving it looking rakishly charming to Ellie's biased gaze. This wouldn't do. She would have to stop finding everything about him so enticing before it was too late.

'Thanks!' she exclaimed in mock outrage. 'I was probably only about twelve at the time.'

'I never had to worry about my weight,' Andrea remarked with a note of self-satisfaction.

'She's improved a lot in certain necessary departments,' Jack agreed with a wolfish grin.

'True,' Ellie confirmed sadly. 'I was depressingly flat-chested for ages. It was the bane of my life.'

'I thought Jack was that,' Luke put in slyly, and Ellie decided that if that was the way he wanted it, she would follow his lead.

'Only because he used to tease me about this whopping crush I used to have on you Luke,' she told him with a smile, then turned to Andrea. 'You know how it is. I thought he was the bees knees, but thankfully that's all over. I discovered there were other fish in the sea, and haven't looked back.'

'Thank God I was spared that particular adolescent nightmare,' Andrea declared with another of her delicate shudders. 'My sister once had a crush—what an awful word—on our music teacher, and it was most unattractive. Thankfully when I told our parents they had him dismissed.'

'That was a bit drastic, wasn't it, considering we all grow out of it. I certainly did,' Ellie protested, and shot Luke an apologetic smile. 'Sorry, Luke, but then you never saw me that way anyway, did you? Which was why Jack told me you were so worried. You didn't want to hurt my feelings.'

That, she was pleased to note, came as quite a jolt to him. Obviously he hadn't expected his brother to say anything to her about the discussion they had had. He preferred to play both sides off against each other from a position of anonymity. His cover had been blown, and he was far from amused, but it only showed in the shadows of his eyes.

'You're family, Ellie. I couldn't bring myself to be blunt. I hoped everything would turn out as I wanted in time, and it did,' he shot back neatly, reminding her, unnecessarily, of their brief affair.

Ellie merely laughed. If he thought to strike a blow, he was way wide of the mark. 'Yes. I'm otherwise engaged, and you have Andrea. What could be better?' she added cheerily and reached for the picnic box. 'Who's for food. I don't know about you lot, but I'm starving.'

It was true too. The days were long gone when Luke could upset her appetite. Andrea helped her serve the food whilst Jack poured out glasses of chilled white wine he took from the cooler. For the next half-hour or so they chatted idly as they ate. When nobody could force down another bite, they packed everything away again.

Satisfyingly full, Ellie stifled a yawn behind her hand. 'Oh, excuse me, but I can hardly keep my eyes open. I'm going to have to have forty winks.'

'You go ahead, Ellie.' Andrea said as she climbed gracefully to her feet and tugged Luke up too. 'Come on, let's go for a walk. I need to burn off some of this food, or I'll be asleep too, and sleeping in the afternoon gives me a headache.' So saying she slipped her arm around his waist and dragged him off with her.

His reluctance made Ellie laugh. 'She's going to lead him a dog's life. It couldn't happen to a nicer guy.'

Jack had been laying on his back with his head resting on his arms. He opened one eye to look at her. 'Do I detect an undercurrent between you and Luke?'

Her thumbs pricked, sensing danger. 'A little. He was rather disparaging about you the other day, and I told him off,' she explained, as ever leaving out the main reason for their antagonism.

His other eye opened. 'Really? What did he say?'

'He called you a chump,' she enlarged, making herself comfortable on her front and shutting her eyes.

'Sounds mild enough to me.'

She stifled another yawn. 'Believe me, he deserved a black eye.'

'So you came rushing to my defence, did you?' Jack sought confirmation, sounding more than a little amused.

'I was the only one there. But even if I wasn't I'd do it again in a second,' she declared forcefully. She looked at him sleepily. 'You're not a chump.'

Jack smiled crookedly. 'Thank you.'

'You're welcome,' she sighed and, closing her eyes again, was asleep in seconds.

Jack stared down at her sleeping form for a long while, his expression sober and thoughtful. Finally he brushed a stray strand of hair away from her mouth then settled himself back down and closed his eyes.

CHAPTER SEVEN

ELLIE sighed and stirred, blinking her eyes carefully against the light. Idly she wondered how long she had been asleep but, from the lack of tightness or stinging on her back, she knew it couldn't have been too long. Nobody was in sight along the whole length of the beach, and only the seagulls disturbed the peace. Turning her head, she saw Jack was still stretched out beside her, and the last misty dregs of sleep vanished.

Careful not to wake him, she came up on her elbow, delighted to have this opportunity to study him unobserved. He was…beautiful. There was no other word for it that came close. How could she have been so blind as not to have seen it before? Was it any wonder she was finding him so very hard to resist.

Everything about him pleased her eye. He was toned and fit and the urge to touch him was as powerful as a magnet. She gave in to it because she really needed to know how he felt. If his skin was as silken as it looked. Very carefully, she reached out and lay her hand on his chest. Her eyes watched his face, seeking signs that he was aware of what she was doing, but there were none. He remained asleep, and she took courage from that and slowly ran her hand back and forth in a gentle caress.

Oh, yes, his skin was silky smooth and yet beneath she could feel the power of his muscles. It was extremely arousing touching him like this, and her teeth closed on her bottom lip as she concentrated on discovering more.

His stomach was flat, with not an ounce of spare flesh to be seen. She scanned its planes once more before her hand slowly progressed lower.

Quick as a flash a hand shot out and caught her wrist, and Ellie gasped, eyes shooting to Jack's face to find him watching her quizzically.

'Go any further and I won't answer for the consequences,' he warned thickly, and her heart lurched.

Ellie made no move to escape, for he wasn't holding her tightly. 'I was just…' She began to explain away her behaviour, but the heat in his gaze dried the words on her tongue.

'I know what you were just… Angel. Believe me, I want to do the same to you,' Jack declared huskily. 'However, making love to you on a public beach wasn't part of the plan.'

Her eyes widened and her throat closed over. 'We weren't making love,' she corrected, but he merely smiled.

'We would have been.'

The part of her that wanted him so badly, knew he was right, but to admit it was out of the question. 'You're taking too much for granted,' she accused him, and in the next instant found herself on her back with Jack looming over her as he rolled, taking her with him.

'I want you, Angel. You can feel that I do,' he told her, and she could feel the surge of his body against hers. 'My control will only get us so far. If you had kept touching me that way, the outcome was inevitable and you know it.'

'I thought you said you would stop if I told you to,' Ellie reminded him, though it was hard to concentrate when they were pressed so very close together and her need of him was a coil of heat inside her.

'I also said you had to mean it. Right now your lips are saying no, but every other inch of you is saying yes. I'm a man, not a saint. I only know you ache for me as much as I ache for you.'

Ellie stared up at him, knowing every word was true. 'This wasn't supposed to happen.'

'I was beginning to think it never would,' Jack breathed as he lowered his head to hers.

'What was that?' Ellie asked half-heartedly, concentrating on the lips so close to her own. If he didn't kiss her soon she might just explode. With a groan she abandoned all pretence of lack of interest. She wanted this—needed it. She would worry about the consequences later. Right now she just knew one thing—she was going out of her mind. 'Never mind. Kiss me, Jack. Please.'

'I'm yours to command,' he groaned back and kissed her.

Ellie sighed with pleasure as his body came to rest on hers and, as if coming home, her arms slipped around his neck, holding on as the kiss stoked the smouldering fires of their mutual passion. Soon, kisses, however passionately erotic, were not enough. Jack abandoned her lips to plunder her neck, and every brush of his lips was like a brand on her sensitised flesh. He forayed lower, seeking the shadowed valley of her breasts with their meagre covering, and Ellie felt her body responding. Her breasts felt tight, her nipples were turgid peaks that ached for his touch, and as if he knew it Jack sought a new target. Her body arched as he brushed the cloth aside and his mouth closed on her. His tongue flicked out, and her muscles clenched as a wave of desire swept through her.

'Jack!' she breathed achingly, needing more than words could say, and it was the sound of her voice that made him go still.

Groaning, Jack buried his face against her for a moment whilst he gathered his control, then he gently replaced the bikini top and looked up at her with eyes darkened by passion.

'You see what I mean? Next time I might not be able to stop,' he confessed, and Ellie licked lips still tender from his kisses.

'Do you know what the worst of it is? I don't think I'd want you to,' she admitted honestly, for there was no way back from here. No point in pretending. Their need was too powerful to be ignored. Only time and distance could cool it, and they had neither.

'What happened to vehement denial?' he asked, but his smile was free of any mockery.

'We just shot it full of holes,' she sighed, her eyes searching his face which had become strangely precious to her in such a short space of time. 'Some holiday this is turning out to be.'

She had come here to lay ghosts, not to find herself caught up in a powerful attraction for a man she thought she hated. Of course she didn't hate him. In fact her feelings for him had undergone a sea change, and become something deeper and warmer. It was all incredibly exciting and intensely alarming at the same time. She didn't mind admitting her intense attraction to him scared her.

'Aren't you having fun?' Jack teased, brushing salty

strands of hair from her forehead. 'That's a pity because I haven't enjoyed myself so much in years.'

'Fun isn't exactly how I would describe what's going on here,' she retorted drily and he smiled.

'What would you call it then?'

'A siege?' she suggested drolly, and Jack chuckled.

'Poor Angel, do you feel bombarded from all sides?'

Ellie scowled at him. 'You're doing your damnedest to undermine my defences right now.'

Blue eyes searched hers. 'Am I succeeding?'

Oh, yes, he was certainly doing that. Her defences were in such a parlous state they barely existed. However, knowing it and saying it were two different things. 'I'll never tell you. Do your worst, but I'm not about to surrender.'

Jack tipped his head on one side. 'You know it's only a matter of time. I will prevail.'

Her lips twitched as she enjoyed the exchange. 'No one could ever accuse you of lacking in confidence.'

'A faint heart never won anything worthwhile.'

She looked at him curiously. 'Am I worth winning?'

Jack shrugged, a smile quirking the corners of his mouth. 'Only time will tell, but I'm willing to take the risk. Come away with me and let's find out,' he suggested next, sending a jolt through her system.

'What? You can't be serious!' Ellie exclaimed attempting to sit up, but he was too heavy to move, so she was forced to lie there blinking at him.

'Never more so,' Jack confirmed. 'I'll hire a boat, then we'll sail down the coast for a couple of days and see what develops. How does that sound?'

She frowned doubtfully. 'It sounds as if you've had too much sun!'

'You think I'm crazy wanting to be alone with you? It sounds eminently sensible to me.'

'Going sailing with you would be too dangerous,' she pronounced huskily.

'You don't trust my sailing ability? I haven't let you drown yet, have I?' he countered and Ellie shot him an old-fashioned look.

'It's not the sailing that bothers me,' she retorted drily and he smiled.

'Worried I'll have my wicked way with you? Well, maybe I will, but only if that's what you want, Ellie. Nothing will happen unless you want it to. So, what's it to be? You know you love getting out on a boat. Can I tempt you?'

He could and that was the major drawback. However, he was right, she did love mucking about on boats. This might be the only opportunity she would get this summer, and she was loath to refuse. So, what to do?

Ellie knew that to agree was to go against all the advice she had given herself about not getting involved with Jack, but the time for non-involvement was long past. She was already involved, but how far and how fast that involvement developed was up to her. She had control, and his offer was tempting. It could do no harm to go, providing she kept her head.

'OK, you've talked me into it,' she told him and, as if he had been waiting on her answer, Jack smiled.

'You won't regret it, I promise you.'

A quirky smile curved her lips. 'I wouldn't get your hopes up too high if I were you. I'm agreeing to the sailing, that's all.'

He laughed huskily. 'I believe you, Angel,' sounding far from convinced.

His reply left her feeling mildly exasperated. 'But you think it's only a matter of time before I end up in your bed, don't you?'

Jack shrugged a shoulder. 'A man has to dream.'

Ellie poked a finger at that shoulder. 'Some dreams become nightmares.' She should know. Her relationship with Luke had been a classic example.

'Whilst other dreams drive the nightmares away,' he countered softly, turning her heart over in the process.

Oh, how she would like that. To have such good memories that the bad ones never returned to haunt her.

'Can anyone join in, or is this a private affair?'

Since neither of them had heard the other couple return, Luke's joking comment from above made them both look up with a start.

Jack held his brother's gaze steadily. 'It's a private affair,' he confirmed lazily, then looked down at Ellie and smiled meaningfully. 'Very private,' he added huskily, then sighed heavily. 'However, as we've been rudely interrupted, we'll have to put it on hold.'

Luke looked hard at Ellie as she and Jack sat up. 'I thought you were going to sleep.'

Jack drew Ellie into the vee of his legs and draped his arms loosely about her. 'We were, but then Ellie decided to seduce me, so sleeping was out of the question,' he returned humorously.

Andrea looked as appalled as Jack had meant her to do. 'You should save that kind of thing until you're somewhere private.'

Ellie couldn't resist responding to that. 'There was nobody here but us and the birds, and they didn't appear to be too bothered. So, what brought you back so soon?'

'Luke started complaining we'd gone too far,' Andrea explained snappily as she sat down.

'Yes, my brother and exercise are only nodding acquaintances,' Jack confirmed. 'He'd rather exercise his charm than his body.'

'I prefer the results,' Luke admitted as he joined them. 'I could never understand how you can inflict pain on yourself and call it fun. But I don't mind watching Andrea working out,' he added, jiggling his eyebrows suggestively at his fiancée. To her patent lack of amusement.

'Honestly Luke, I'm not a peep-show. You'd be fitter if you joined me,' Andrea pointed out, but Luke pulled a face and stretched out comfortably.

'Too much like hard work, darling.'

'Perhaps I ought to work out,' Ellie suggested, leaning back against Jack and casting a look up at him through her lashes.

'I love your body the way it is,' he told her silkily. 'In fact, I'd love to love your body any place any time.'

'Oh, pl...ease!' Luke exclaimed disgustedly. 'There's a time and place for everything.'

'We know. That's why Ellie and I are going off for a few days,' Jack revealed casually and, as Ellie's nerves jolted at the unexpected revelation, Luke's head shot up.

'What was that? You're going away? Where?'

'I'm hiring a boat. We're going to sail down the coast,' his brother obligingly explained.

Luke scooted round into a sitting position. 'Sounds like fun. We could go with you,' he suggested, and everyone looked at him in surprise.

Andrea was far from amused. 'Don't be silly, Luke. You know I hate boats,' she chided him. 'Besides, it's obvious they want to be alone. Two's company, four's a crowd. I think it's a great idea.'

To everyone's amazement, Luke promptly jumped to his feet. 'You wouldn't know a great idea if it bit you!' he exclaimed and stormed off.

Stunned, Andrea stared after him. 'Well, really!' she said, then rose with a set look to her face. 'He's been acting like a bear with a sore head for days, but that doesn't give him the right to speak to me like that!' she declared wrathfully, and went after him.

Ellie blew out a silent whistle. 'That went down well.'

'If I didn't know better, I'd say he was jealous,' Jack declared, frowning at his brother's disappearing back.

Ellie's heart skipped a beat as he came perilously close to the truth. Luke *was* jealous. Jealous that she could prefer anyone over him. Luke was backing himself into a pretty tight corner. If he wasn't careful he was going to be found out, and then the fat would surely be in the fire. When that happened he was likely to take his anger out on her. The woman he considered the source of the problem.

'There's never been anything for him to be jealous about,' she insisted, made distinctly uneasy by his behaviour.

'True, but he certainly doesn't like seeing us together. Now why should that be?' Jack mused and, because she didn't like the way his thoughts were turning, Ellie attempted to change tack.

'Maybe he doesn't think you're good for me.'

Jack tipped his head down and grinned lazily. 'What do you think?'

Looking up at him, Ellie felt an unexpected surge of emotion swell inside her. What did she think? There was no question of it. He was good for her. Oh so very good. Just days ago she would have thought differently, but she knew him better now. He wasn't the man she thought he was. These past days had shown her that. He was turning into someone she enjoyed being with. No, looked forward to being with. Not because he could turn her on with just a look, but because he made her feel good about herself. She was happy when she was with him, in a way she had never been happy with anyone else.

She smiled wistfully. 'I wish I hadn't been so blind all these years. I've missed being friends with you, Jack.'

He sighed heavily. 'It would have been more pleasant, but I have to admit I don't feel very friendly towards you now, Angel.'

Her brows rose at the flirtatious comment, and she admitted to herself that flirting with him was becoming addictive. 'No?'

Jack shook his head. 'No. Now I want you as a lover. I want the woman you are, not the child you were. I want your passion, your fire,' he told her with a depth of emotion that tightened invisible fingers about her heart. 'Nothing less will do. Does that scare you?'

It ought to. Lord knew, it should have—but it didn't. His words touched a core in her that she hadn't known existed. She knew she wanted nothing less from him. The knowledge filled her mind with wonder. She didn't know why she felt this so strongly, she only knew she did.

'Nothing about you scares me, Jack,' she told him boldly. 'But that doesn't mean I'm going to fall at your feet and say: take me I'm yours!'

Jack's eyes danced, and his smile was rueful. 'I always knew you'd be hell on wheels when you realised your full potential. Come on, we'd better go after the others and check that war hasn't broken out. I need to make a phone call about the boat, too,' he said, climbing to his feet and holding out a hand to help her up. 'With any luck I can arrange to have it tomorrow.'

That would be fine by her. If Luke was throwing a tantrum, she didn't want to be anywhere in the vicinity. Besides, she was secretly looking forward to being alone with Jack, despite the temptation he presented. Which only went to prove what a crazy world it was. She had been obsessed with Luke all those years, and never felt this depth of need or urgency. Which underlined how foundationless her feelings for him had been. If she had only known then what she knew now... But hindsight was a perverse thing. It showed you where you had gone wrong, but not the way to change anything.

That evening Ellie made a head start on her packing, gathering together the things she would need for a few days at sea, for they would be leaving early the following morning. Jack had managed to arrange to borrow a yacht from a friend and they would have the use of it for as long as they wanted. There was a fluttery feeling in her stomach at the prospect of being alone with him—totally alone—for the first time, but anxiety had little to do with it. She knew the feeling was anticipation. She wanted this time with Jack more than she could remember wanting anything for a long time.

Her packing was interrupted by a soft knock on the door and, when she went to open it, she found her mother outside. There was a tiny frown of concern on the older woman's forehead that caused Ellie to step aside to allow her mother in.

'Jack tells me you're going away for a few days,' Mary Thornton said without preamble as Ellie closed the door. Her gaze went to the open bag on the bed which mutely confirmed her statement.

Ellie wondered what was coming. Her mother hadn't looked this serious for a long time. 'Yes, we are. He's borrowed a boat. I'm hoping we can take in Naples. I want to see the Farnese collection again,' she responded as she turned to the chest of drawers.

Mary Thornton sat on the bed and watched her daughter sort through a pile of underwear. 'Is that wise, darling?'

Ellie tucked her finds into the bag and blew her hair out of her eyes. 'Well, I don't think they're cursed, so I should be safe enough,' she returned mischievously.

'You know perfectly well what I meant, Ellie,' Mary Thornton advised, shortly, and Ellie sighed.

'OK, I know what you mean, and no I don't think it unwise. We'll only be gone a couple of days.'

'You don't think going away with Jack is a little…premature?' her mother suggested and Ellie flushed, fully aware of what her mother meant by 'going away'.

'We're going sailing, nothing more,' she insisted, although she couldn't guarantee that that was how it would stay. Passions were running high between her and Jack, and that meant anything could happen.

'Sit down a moment, Ellie,' Mary commanded gently, and Ellie reluctantly sank onto the bed. 'Darling, are you in love with Jack?'

The question sent a jolt of electricity through Ellie's system, jangling her nerves and increasing the beat of her heart. 'What sort of question is that?' she gasped, not sure whether to laugh or not.

'A serious one, and I would like an answer please.'

There was a note in Mary Thornton's voice which her daughter well remembered from her childhood. It meant she had better give a straight answer. 'No, I'm not in love with Jack,' she said, but the minute the answer left her lips, she felt a strange queasiness settle in her stomach. 'I like him a lot. We like each other a lot,' she added hastily.

'Of course you do. Anyone can see that. The pair of you create enough wattage to light the island!' Mary agreed wryly. 'But...'

'But?' Ellie pursued, wondering what was coming next in this already startling interview.

Mary sighed and reached out to take her daughter's hand. 'Do have a care, darling. I know you wouldn't want to hurt a soul, but Jack's...vulnerable.'

Ellie was so surprised, she couldn't say anything for a moment or two. She had thought her mother was going to warn her about getting hurt by Jack, not warn her of hurting him! 'What are you trying to tell me, Mum?'

Her mother looked worried and uncomfortable by turns, but after a moment's hesitation she carried on. 'Don't allow him to think you feel more for him than you do, Ellie. Be kind.'

Ellie frowned, trying to make sense of the admonition, but failing. There was some hidden message here. Her mother knew she wouldn't deliberately hurt anyone, but why did she have to take care with Jack? It was a moment or two before a possible reason suddenly occurred to her. She thought she saw the light.

'Does this have something to do with the woman Jack

is in love with?' she asked, and her mother looked surprised.

'You know about her?'

'Jack told me,' Ellie nodded, certain she was on the right track.

'I see,' Mary Thornton said slowly.

'How do you know about her?' her daughter asked in turn, and Mary took a steadying breath, shifting about nervously before answering.

'He confided in me a long time ago,' she confirmed.

'You know who she is?' Ellie's curiosity was piqued.

Mary Thornton gave her daughter a steady look. 'I do, but don't ask me more, for I won't break a confidence. All I wanted to say was that whatever happens between you, don't play games with him. Be honest. Don't pretend what you don't feel. He's a good man and he deserves some good fortune for a change.'

Ellie had never guessed that her mother was so protective towards Jack, but it really shouldn't surprise her. She had taken the three motherless boys under her wing when she married their father and loved them unquestioningly. Jack's abortive love affair must have hurt him, and her mother knew it. Which was why she was warning her daughter not to cause him any more grief.

'I won't do anything to hurt him, Mum. Why would you think I would?'

Her mother captured both of her hands and squeezed them encouragingly. 'Because my darling, when it comes to men, you tend to go overboard. Look how you convinced yourself you were in love with Luke, and you weren't. Now, Luke being the type of man he is, that would not have hurt him in the long run, but Jack's another matter. He can be hurt. Think on that, darling, and be the gentle loving woman I know you can be.'

Ellie winced at the unwelcome reminder of her stupidity. Thank goodness her mother didn't know the true depth of it. As it was, what she did know was bad enough. 'I know I was foolish about Luke, but that's in the past. I've grown up—finally,' she added wryly, and Mary Thornton gave her a hug.

'I didn't mean to make you feel bad. I just thought you might not realise the damage you could do. I spoke from the best of intentions, for I do so want you both to be happy. Now I'll leave you to finish your packing,' she said as she rose and crossed to the door. There she paused and shot her daughter an impish grin. 'It doesn't sound very responsible and motherly to hope you enjoy yourself, when you're planning to spend a torrid few days alone with a handsome man, does it?' she laughed.

'Hey, it's going to be a totally innocent sailing trip!' Ellie exclaimed, not quite knowing how to respond without confirming the suggestion.

Mary laughed louder. 'And the moon is made of green cheese! I wasn't born yesterday you know. I had my moments. Your father and I…well, maybe I'd better save that for another day!' she tantalised as she went out, leaving her daughter in a state of bemusement.

What an amazing conversation! In a roundabout way, her mother had just given her blessing to whatever may or may not develop between her and Jack. Providing she didn't hurt him. Ellie shook her head in wonderment. It was hard to believe what had just been said.

Could her mother really be suggesting Jack could fall for her, given the right encouragement? It hardly seemed possible. Yet her mother seemed convinced he was vulnerable. She couldn't say she had seen any signs of it. They wanted each other, that was all. Any deeper feelings were out of the question. Jack knew that as well as she did.

Clearly her mother was overreacting because of what had happened in the past. This was different. There was no love involved, only passion. Jack wasn't about to fall for her nor she for him. Which was exactly the way she wanted it...wasn't it?

That was the question. Did she really know what she did want? Once it had seemed so clear, but now... The seed of doubt, once sown, took root, and slowly began to germinate in the recesses of her mind.

CHAPTER EIGHT

By LATE afternoon of the following day they were sailing steadily round the coast towards Salerno. Jack had promised they would drop in at Naples on the return trip. Now Ellie had the wheel whilst Jack dealt with the sails. She loved the feel of spray on her cheeks and the breeze in her hair, and felt like laughing for the sheer joy of it. Up ahead, Jack whistled happily. In deck shoes, black shorts and white T-shirt, he looked good enough to eat. Her heart did a crazy flip-flop in her chest and, for no reason at all, she started smiling.

'Something amusing you?' Jack asked as he made his way back and jumped down beside her.

'I was just thinking how handsome you looked,' she admitted and something flickered in his eyes.

'Now that deserves a kiss,' he responded and bent his head quickly, taking her lips in a short but nerve-tingling caress. Drawing back, he looked into her slightly dreamy eyes. 'Hungry?'

Ellie's stomach tightened as the glowing embers of desire sparked into life at the teasing question. Feeling reckless, she responded in kind. 'Depends what's on the menu.'

Laughing, he checked their heading before answering. 'Me or cold chicken and salad.'

'Mmm, decisions, decisions,' she teased back. 'What do I really fancy? I know. I'll have the chicken now and save you for later. I've a feeling you'll improve with time.'

'Like a good wine,' Jack agreed, and she grinned.

'Or a ripe old cheese,' she riposted with a giggle.

Jack tipped his head as he watched her. 'You should do that more often,' he said, and she looked a query.

'What, call you an old cheese?'

Blue eyes narrowed playfully. 'No, laugh. You didn't look too happy at Christmas.'

She hadn't been, for she had been forced to follow a lead she was uncomfortable with. 'I probably had a lot on my mind.'

'You should have come to me for help,' Jack remarked, and she shook her head with a wry smile.

'You were the last person I would have turned to then,' she said wryly.

He picked up on the qualification. 'Then? Does that mean you'd turn to me now?' he asked curiously and Ellie sighed.

'Yes, I probably would,' she confirmed with a smile, and Jack nodded, his expression a curious mixture of satisfaction and something else.

'Good. Hold this course, there's a bay coming up we can spend the night in—unless you want to head for civilisation?'

Ellie darted him a quick look, knowing whatever she decided now would be important. If she told him to head for the nearest village, she would be saying keep your distance, and he would respect that. But, if she was honest with herself, she didn't want to say that at all. She wanted him, with a need that seemed to be growing daily. Why was she denying them what they both wanted? It was the fear that she was making another mistake. She had trusted Luke and he had used her. Yet Jack was everything Luke was not. Honest, strong, kind, trustworthy. He had said he wouldn't let anything bad happen to her, and she believed him. An affair with Jack need not be a mistake. It was time to take a risk.

'The bay sounds perfect,' she said huskily, and then the strangest thing happened. The instant her decision was made, all doubt seemed to vanish. Something inside her said this was right. That nothing which involved Jack would be wrong. She had never felt so sure of anything in her life before.

Jack said nothing just nodded but, as he passed her, he touched her briefly on the shoulder. It was the merest caress, yet it made her feel warm and bubbly inside and brought a smile to her lips.

She turned and looked after him in a kind of wonder, searching for what it was about him that made the difference, but he was just Jack. No different from the man who had plagued her life with his criticisms. It was she who had changed, seeing things as they really were, not how she had thought them to be. Which meant the man she had thought she loved, she now disliked, and the man she had hated, she now lov... The thought ended abruptly as she realised just what she was saying, but it couldn't be true. No, no, that was absurd.

Ellie turned her concentration back to sailing the yacht, feeling confused and unsettled. She wasn't going to think along those lines. She wanted Jack in a passionate way, but that was all. That had to be all.

They sailed on for another hour, then dropped anchor in the tiny secluded bay. Whilst Jack stowed the sails, Ellie, once more in control of her thoughts, went below and began preparing the food. As Jack had promised there was chicken and salad, plus wine and other tasty tidbits the housekeeper had supplied for their trip. They certainly weren't going to starve.

She was cutting bread into chunky wedges when Jack called down to her.

'I'm going for a swim before supper. Care to join me?'

Ellie didn't even have to think about it. She abandoned the bread and headed for the steps. The thought of a cool swim after the heat of the day was music to her ears. She had been wearing her bikini under her shorts and T-shirt, and it was the work of a moment to strip them off when she was back on deck. Jack was already down to the minuscule trunks he preferred to wear for swimming, and as ever the sight of so much tanned, muscular flesh set her pulse tripping along.

Jack didn't miss the way her eyes ate him up, and it brought a sultry look to his eyes. 'Of course, we don't have to swim if you'd rather do something else,' he suggested but, tempting as the offer was, Ellie shook her head.

'I think we've got time for a swim as well,' she pointed out with a quirky grin.

'As well as what?' he queried, and she laughed.

'Why, supper, of course. What else?'

Blue eyes glittered dangerously. 'So that's how it's going to be, is it? Something tells me I'm going to have to assert my authority or you'll be walking all over me,' Jack declared, advancing on her.

Her brows rose, though she was careful to retreat. 'Oh, yes, and how do you propose to do that?' she wanted to know, just as her legs struck the side.

'Like this,' Jack grinned, and swooping he picked her up in his arms and promptly tossed her over the side.

Ellie just had time to take a deep breath before she disappeared under the water. Arching her body, she gave a quick flick of her feet and shot to the surface. Brushing the hair from her eyes, she trod water and glanced round. Jack surfaced a few feet away, still grinning.

She shook her head at him. 'Bad move, Jack. Very bad move. You'll pay for that.'

'Threats, Angel?' Jack mocked, slowly beginning to circle her.

'Promises,' she countered. 'You're going to be sorry.'

'Mmm, can't wait,' he laughed softly, and she smiled back.

'What do you imagine I'm going to do to you?'

'Plenty—with any luck.'

Ellie circled too, maintaining the distance between them. 'It's supposed to be a penance. You aren't supposed to enjoy it!'

That brought another of those sultry smiles he did so well. 'I doubt very much if there is anything you could do that I wouldn't enjoy, so do your worst, Angel.'

'You don't think I could hurt you?' she taunted, though she knew she wouldn't even attempt to. It wasn't in her nature to be deliberately cruel.

'Not physically, no,' Jack agreed, and she frowned.

'But I could hurt you in other ways?' she probed, no longer teasing. 'Mum hinted the same last night.'

'Really?' Jack sobered too, and looked around him. He pointed to some rocks not far off. 'Let's go sit over there, then you can tell me what she said.'

He set off using a long lazy stroke that got him to the rock just ahead of her. Climbing out he reached down to help her up. The rock was still warm, and Ellie stretched out, enjoying the early evening sun. Jack made himself comfortable resting on his elbow looking down at her.

'So, what did Mary have to say about me?'

Sighing, Ellie looked up at him. A lock of damp hair had fallen over his forehead, and she reached up to comb it back, and even that small gesture made her fingertips tingle. She debated whether to tell him the truth or not, but knew she didn't want to lie to him if she could help it. There were too many lies already. 'She asked me not to hurt you.'

Jack's brows shot up, registering his surprise. 'How does she imagine you would do that?' he asked, capturing her hand and linking his fingers with hers.

Their connected hands were sending a wave of heat up her arm, centring deep inside her. 'It had to do with the woman you love. She was worried that I might...mislead you into thinking I feel more for you than I do.'

Understanding flashed in his eyes, and a rueful smile curved his lips. 'I see. She needn't worry. I know exactly what you feel for me.'

Her eyes rounded, and her heart knocked suddenly. 'You do?'

'Oh, yes. You want me.'

For no reason at all, the answer made her throat close over. It was so bald—so lacking in any kind of warmth. She felt disappointed for some reason, and it must have showed on her face.

'Unless I missed something?' Jack queried, and Ellie slowly shook her head.

'No. No, you didn't,' she confirmed, but there was a

nagging feeling inside her that something was wrong. She just didn't know what.

'So, is that all she had to say?'

Dragging herself away from her muddled thoughts, Ellie produced a grin. 'Actually she wanted to make sure I knew what I was doing, going away for a torrid few days with you.'

He laughed and smiled lazily. 'Torrid, hmm? Well, do you?'

There was that certain something in his smile which set her heart tripping. 'Oh, I think so.'

Some emotion flashed into his eyes, but was quickly hidden. 'You can always change your mind, Angel. I've never compelled a woman to do anything against her better judgement, and I don't intend to start with you.'

'Would you be disappointed if I did?'

'Very. I've been looking forward to this.'

'Then it's just as well I have no intention of backing out,' she told him, holding his gaze so that he would be in no doubt. Then, quick as a flash, she pulled her hand from his and gave him a shove. As he fell backwards, she jumped to her feet and shot him a grin. 'Race you back,' she challenged and dived in.

Ellie was a decent swimmer but, even giving herself a head start, she knew he would soon catch her up, which he did when she was no more than halfway back to the boat. Jack was waiting on deck to help her up the ladder when she climbed out of the water.

'I should tan your hide for that,' he threatened, wrapping a towel around her, but instead of drying her off, he used it to haul her closer.

Ellie placed her hands flat against his chest and looked up at him. 'Is that really what you want to do?' she asked breathlessly, knowing it wasn't from the aroused state of his body. Feeling his desire for her set her own body pulsing with need.

He didn't answer, instead his head swooped and he took her mouth in a kiss that demanded a response. She gave it, welcoming the sensual thrust of his tongue, matching it with her own. He touched her in no other place and, for sheer eroticism, it was mind-blowing. It was a greedy, hungry kiss that fed off its own passion and left her aching when he finally lifted his head.

Without a word Jack dropped the towel and picked her up in his arms. Equally speechless, Ellie wrapped her arms around his neck and buried her face against his shoulder. She had thought he was taking her to the main cabin, but instead he set her down beside him in the shower. He disposed of their clothes in a few brisk moves then clean water was washing away the sticky salt. Ellie closed her eyes as he turned her so her back was to him and ran soapy hands over her sensitised skin, gasping when he found her breasts, then groaning when he abandoned them again to trail lower. It was delicious torture, but she couldn't allow him to have it all his own way. Turning, she took the soap and proceeded to give him a taste of his own medicine. It was music to her ears to hear him catch his breath as her hands roved over the muscled planes of his chest but, when she attempted to go further, his hands fastened on her wrists. Their eyes met.

'I only have so much control,' he growled, reaching past her to turn off the water. Then he was picking her up again, this time heading for the bedroom.

Jack dropped her damp body on the bed and followed her down, one powerful male thigh settling between her own. Ellie groaned with satisfaction as his body moulded itself to hers. This was what she had ached for ever since she had set eyes on him again, and her arms went round him, her hands caressing every inch of silky male flesh she could reach. Jack's hand stroked in one long scorching caress from her shoulder to thigh then back again as his lips plundered the sensitive skin of her neck.

When his mouth trailed lower to the soft foothills of her breasts, Ellie caught her breath, waiting for the touch she longed for. Yet it was not his lips which claimed the peak, but his hand and, when she blinked her eyes open and looked down, it was to find him watching her through eyes heavy with barely controlled passion. As her breathing grew more ragged she watched him look down to where his thumb was grazing her turgid flesh, teasing her nipple into a hard nub. Pleasure arced through her, down to the aching centre of her passion, and helplessly her body arched upwards, seeking more. Jack's head bent, his tongue flickered out, and as she cried out his mouth closed hotly around her flesh, suckling her towards the point of insanity. Ellie's fingers blindly sought the dark tangle of his hair and clung on as she was battered by delicious sensations. When he transferred his attention to her other breast, a low moan was forced from her throat as he dealt it the same nerve-tingling pleasure.

'Oh, Jack,' she sighed, but got no further because he was moving on.

Hands framing her hips, he laid a trail of kisses down her body. His tongue found her navel and circled it lazily before pressing onwards, past the curve of her hips until he reached the juncture of her thighs. There, with the gentle pressure of his hands, he urged her to open to

him, and with infinite care his lips and tongue sought
and found the moist core of her. Ellie's fingers clutched
at the covers beneath her as Jack's deft caresses ravaged
her senses, tightening the spiralling coil inside and
brought her to a swift climax.

As she lay trembling in the aftermath, Jack came up
beside her. Taking his weight on his arms, he settled
himself between her thighs and looked down at her.

'That's what I wanted to do,' he growled huskily,
dropping ever more passionate kisses on her mouth.
'You were so sweet, so responsive, I nearly lost it,' he
confessed.

Instead he had made sure that she did. Ellie had never
known such an unselfish lover, a man intent on giving
a woman pleasure before taking his own. It was a revelation. She held on to his shoulders, not really surprised
to feel the desire mounting in her again so soon.

'I wanted us to lose it together,' she breathed, kissing
him back, and felt his lips curve.

'We will, Angel. We will,' he declared and began to
make love to her all over again.

This time they each took it in turns to arouse the other.
Limbs entangled, they rolled back and forth across the
bed, lips and hands driving each other crazy. The silence
of the cabin was punctuated only by their moans and
sighs of pleasure and their pleas for more. Ellie moved
beneath Jack restlessly and there was an urgency to their
caresses which was fast breaking the bounds of their
control. Their sweat-slick bodies were burning up with
need, and she knew that if he did not end this soon, she
would die.

'Please, Jack, now!' she urged brokenly, and with a

groan his hands fastened on her hips lifting her to receive him.

With one powerful thrust he was home, and through her own sense of satisfaction at having him buried so deep within her, she could feel him battling for control. Yet control was the last thing she wanted. She wanted his passion and she wanted it now. Locking her legs around him, she moved against him in an invitation that destroyed the last vestiges of restraint.

Groaning, he began to move, every thrust driving them ever nearer to the goal they sought. There was no thought of holding back on either part. Then she was there, reaching heaven and shooting out into space on an explosion of pleasure that had her crying out. Seconds later Jack joined her, and all they could do was hold on to each other and ride the waves of passion until they reached the safety of the farther shore and came to rest.

Spent though he was, Jack's hand came up to gently cup her flushed cheek. 'Eleanora,' he sighed softly, and for the first time ever the name sounded beautiful to her ears.

Ellie found the energy to comb her fingers into his sweat-damp hair, sighing with a profound sense of satisfaction. What had just happened was…indescribable. She had reached peaks she hadn't known it was possible to climb. Jack had taken her there in a way she knew no other man ever could.

She knew that it signified something important, but her eyes felt as if they had lead weights in them. Sleep was calling her, and she didn't have the strength to fight it. Closing her eyes, she wrapped her other arm around him. She would think about whatever it was tomorrow.

* * *

It was dark when she woke, and she was alone in the bed. Coming up on one elbow, the cover which had been draped over her fell away. Jack must have covered her over when he left. She could hear noises coming from the galley and it made her realise that she was hungry too. Clambering from the bed, she gathered a brightly coloured sarong from the chair where she had left it and wrapped it around herself before padding out to find him.

Jack was indeed in the galley and, having arrived unheard, Ellie leaned against the doorframe and watched him. He was setting out the salad ingredients she had sorted earlier, on a tray, whistling tunelessly to himself as he bustled about. A fond smile curved her lips as she noted he was eating as much as he was putting on the plates.

'Hi,' she greeted softly, and he looked up with a start, his surprise turning to a look of pleasure when he saw her.

Wiping his hands on the shorts he had put on, he took the few steps necessary to join her. 'Hi, yourself,' he returned, taking her chin between finger and thumb and raising her head so that he could kiss her thoroughly. There was a warmth in his eyes when he raised his head that matched the glow in her chest.

Ellie's hands had gone to his waist to steady herself, and now she slid them slowly up his chest. 'I missed you,' she confessed as he pulled her into his arms and hugged her close.

'I planned to be back before you woke. This was supposed to be a midnight snack,' he said, inclining his head towards the food.

'Is it midnight?' she asked in surprise and he grinned.

'It's closer to two in the morning. I didn't intend to sleep so long, but you wore me out.'

Her eyes danced. 'Perhaps we ought to limit the amount of loving you get,' she suggested.

'Don't even think about it,' Jack rejected the idea immediately. 'Are you hungry?'

There was no doubt this time he was referring to food. 'Famished,' she confessed, and her stomach growled to add the full stop to it.

Jack picked up the tray. 'Do you want to eat up on deck? It's still warm out there.'

'Oh, up top. No question,' she decided and led the way outside.

They sat out under the stars, Jack leaning back against the seat and Ellie leaning on him. For a while they said very little as they quickly demolished the chicken and salad. Only when her initial hunger was satisfied did Ellie sit back with a sigh.

'You know, I never thought we'd end up like this,' she mused, picking up an apple and taking a bite out of it.

'On a boat?' Jack teased, and she elbowed him in the ribs, causing him to grunt at the unexpected impact.

'No, as lovers,' Ellie corrected as Jack fastened his arms about her waist, his chin coming to rest on the cushion of her hair.

'Strange things happen at sea,' he joked and she groaned at the tired adage.

'That isn't what I mean.'

It might not be the most appropriate time to talk about his brother, but the truth was beginning to weigh on her conscience now that she and Jack were involved. Never mind her pride. He ought to know, and she should be the one to tell him.

'Luke was always between us. I think we need to talk about him, Jack.'

'No, we don't,' Jack denied forcefully, angling her head so that he could look down into her eyes. 'I'm declaring this boat a Luke-free zone. This is our time, Angel. I don't want to think about anything but us. Forget Luke.'

She probably ought to have insisted, but the intensity of his gaze caused her to back off. It was incredibly heady to know he wanted nothing to intrude into their private world, and as a consequence she could do nothing but comply. 'OK,' she breathed. 'No Luke. He wasn't the only reason I never saw us as lovers anyway,' she went on huskily.

'No?'

Maybe she couldn't tell him the truth, but she could hint at it. 'My last relationship wasn't a happy experience,' she confided, and that was putting it mildly, but was all she could tell him about her and Luke. 'I made up my mind I wasn't going to get involved again for a long time.' Especially not with another Thornton.

'So why are you here with me?' he wanted to know, and she sighed.

'I couldn't resist you. Oh, I tried, but in the end I just didn't want to fight it any longer.'

'Which was what I was hoping for,' Jack responded, planting a kiss on her hair.

Ellie finished her apple and tossed the core onto the tray. 'So you have your wish. What happens now?' Only as she asked the question did she realise how important it was for her to know where she stood. She had to know what his intentions were now.

'Who knows,' Jack shrugged. 'We're at the beginning of something even I don't know the end of. I do know I'm in no rush to get there.'

That was good. She needed to hear that, but... 'How long do your affairs usually last?' she asked, and from the way he went still, she could sense him frowning.

'You make it sound as if I've had hundreds of affairs.'

'Maybe that's an exaggeration, but you've had more than me. I just wanted to get some idea as to how quickly you get bored.'

'That would rather depend on the woman. You can breathe easy, Angel. You haven't bored me yet,' he returned sardonically.

'That's a comfort,' Ellie quipped back wryly. They had been lovers for only a few hours, so the gloss was hardly likely to have worn off.

'You're worrying too much. Can't you just accept that we're here together now?' Jack suggested, and she knew that she was being foolish. There were no guarantees on relationships such as theirs. Passion that sprang up so swiftly, could just as easily vanish overnight. The sensible thing to do was enjoy it while it lasted—however short a time that might prove to be.

Ellie tugged at his hands until he relaxed his grip then twisted in his arms. Coming up on her knees, she straddled his legs and placed her hands on his shoulders. 'You're right. I'm just being silly. Put it down to the fact that nobody has ever made me feel the way that you do, and it's made me a tad paranoid about losing it.'

Jack's hands had come to rest on her thighs, and now began a slow glide upwards to her hips. Fastening on her slim behind, he urged her closer to him, so that she could feel the stirrings of his arousal. 'I told you this wasn't going to go away. Trust me, we have plenty of time,' he told her with that wicked glint in his eye that set her heart tripping faster.

Her own response was instant, her body coming alive again as desire quickened in the core of her. Holding his gaze, she moved against him, and was delighted when he let out a soft groan.

'Minx,' he accused her, and she laughed huskily.

'You never asked me if I got bored easily,' she told him, still moving against him, and arousing herself as much as him, so that she had to bite down on her lip to withhold a moan of her own.

Jack's hands trailed up her ribcage, his thumbs finding the slopes of her breasts and gliding up them to the stiffening peaks. 'God, I hope not, I want you too much.'

Ellie's head went back as his hands claimed her breasts, her fingers clamping onto the flesh of his shoulders. When she looked down at him again, her eyes were clouded with need. 'Perhaps we can keep boredom at bay between us. Want to give it a try?'

His smile was wolfish. 'I'm game for anything,' he declared, and that was all the encouragement she needed to untie the knot of her sarong and let it fall to the floor.

Eyes flashing a warning of her intent, she lowered her head and found one flat male nipple, teasing it with her tongue and teeth until she forced another groan from him, then she transferred her attention to its mate, dealing it the same fate. When she had gained the same result, she raised her head, tossing her hair back so that she could look into his eyes.

'Are you still with me?' she taunted and he laughed.

'Angel, I'm way ahead of you.'

Her fingers fluttered down to the fastening of his shorts and hovered there, 'Do you want me to stop?'

Jack shook his head, eyes dancing with amusement, yet behind it was a burning desire. 'You do, and I might just be forced to do something desperate.'

Ellie flicked open the snap. 'Well now, we can't allow that to happen, can we?' she said laughingly, and very very slowly began to lower the zip.

'Were you a torturer in a former life?' Jack groaned, raising his hips as she tugged the offending shorts down. He barely had time to kick them aside before her hand closed around him and her head lowered. Then he had to grit his teeth as he watched her doing to him what he had done to her earlier.

Ellie had no intention of going too far, but Jack stopped her anyway by tangling his fingers in her hair and bringing her head up to his. 'Hey!' she protested gruffly.

'Enough,' he ordered, rolling sideways and taking her with him so that she ended up beneath him. With one smooth move he was sheathed inside her once more. Braced above her, he looked down into her flushed face. 'Witch. What you do to me! I can't get enough of you.'

Ellie reached up and pulled his head down to hers, taking his mouth. 'Last I heard, rationing was over,' she breathed and he groaned.

'Thank God for that,' he muttered and kissed her.

It was the last intelligible thing either said for some considerable time.

CHAPTER NINE

THE three days that followed were, in Ellie's opinion, magical. They just sailed down the coast and back again, only putting into a harbour when their supplies finally ran low. The remainder of the time they spent together, either talking, swimming or, most often, making love.

If she had thought that by becoming lovers, the desire they had for each other would begin to lessen, she was mistaken. In fact, the opposite happened. The more they made love, the deeper the need grew. Ellie had never experienced such an empathy with another human being. It was as if she had found a lost part of herself. Jack made her feel complete for the first time in her life.

She was happy.

On the third day, as promised, they stopped off at Naples so that Ellie could see the Farnese collection. The paintings were magnificent, and she could have spent hours wandering around, studying them from all angles. Eventually, they were forced to leave because the museum was closing. They stayed on in the city for dinner and ate at a harbour-side restaurant noted for its seafood and relaxed dress code, and lingered over coffee. Consequently, it was quite late before they finally returned to the yacht.

'Do we really have to go back tomorrow?' Ellie asked as she emerged from the shower with a towel wrapped around her, using another to dry her hair.

Jack had already showered, and was lounging on the

bed. He rose, leaving the towel he wore hitched low on his hips. He took the towel from her and continued the job of drying her hair. ''Fraid so. It's the engagement party tomorrow night, remember?'

She grimaced. 'I'd forgotten. I must have had other things on my mind,' she returned wickedly, and he laughed.

'Such as?' he probed, casting the towel aside and combing his fingers through the damp gold strands.

His touch on her scalp sent shivers down her spine. 'Oh, I'd guess it would be six foot odd of handsome, sexy male.'

'Been thinking about me, Angel?'

Only all the time, she acknowledged wryly. 'Now and again,' she told him with an offhand shrug. 'You know, when I can't find a good book to read.'

'Are you telling me I'm not as interesting as a book?' Jack growled, and she giggled.

'I would never be so rude,' she denied, eyes dancing as she waited for his response to that. 'But you are closer to forty than I am. You can't expect to be as…vigorous as you once were.'

'That does it,' Jack declared menacingly. 'Nobody questions my manhood. Especially not a little squirt like you,' he added, spinning her around. 'Apologise or take the consequences.'

Ellie looked up at him from beneath her lashes, nerves thrilling to the glint in his eye. 'I can't. It's against my religion.'

Teeth flashed whitely as he smiled wolfishly. 'Then I guess I'm going to have to show you how wrong you are,' he pronounced, swinging her up in his arms and carrying her to the bed.

A long time later, Ellie lay in Jack's arms and smiled. 'I take it back. You're much better than a book,' she said, running her hand in lazy circles over his chest.

'And my manhood?' Jack queried.

'Is in good working order, I'm happy to say.'

'Good. Let that be a lesson to you,' he retorted, and she could feel the rumble of laughter in his chest.

'You know, there are some lessons that have to be repeated often for the message to get through,' she teased. 'You might have to jog my memory from time to time.'

'It will be my pleasure, Angel. Now get some rest, we have an early start tomorrow.'

Ellie frowned, wishing he hadn't reminded her of why they had to leave early. She had been trying not to think about it ever since he had brought up the subject of the party over dinner. A cloud had appeared on her horizon, because it had dawned on her that time was running out—literally. She had realised that by going back, the end of the pretence was approaching.

The thought of it then, as now, made her go cold inside, yet there was no avoiding the truth. After the party it would only be a matter of a few days before she had to go home, and she knew what would happen then. The real world would impinge on this magical one she inhabited. Icy fingers tightened on her heart as she accepted the blunt truth of it. Jack had his own life to live and so did she. However real this was here, it didn't exist in their other lives.

Which was a problem because she didn't want it to end. The imminence of their departure was forcing her to be honest with herself. It was too soon. She wanted more. She wasn't ready to end it. Yet it had only ever been a ruse. OK, the affair had become real, but nothing else was. It was a game, never meant to be taken seriously. Not that she was taking it seriously exactly, she just didn't want it to end so soon. Yet there was nothing she could do to change things.

She sighed heavily, feeling foolishly close to tears. Which was ridiculous because she had always known it was a game. It just didn't feel like one, that was all.

'What's up?' Jack asked softly.

There was no way she was going to tell him why she suddenly felt so maudlin. She was going to be as civilised about it as he would be. 'Oh, nothing really. I just don't want to go back tomorrow—or is it today now?' She didn't know what time it was, but it had to be after midnight. 'Do you think they'd miss us if we played truant?' she tried to make light of it but didn't sound too convincing to her own ears.

Jack's hand caressed the curve of her shoulder. 'It's a tempting thought, but we'd never get away with it. Your mother and my father would have plenty to say. Much as I'd rather sail off into the sunset with you, we'll have to go back.'

She knew he was right. 'Oh, well, they say all good things come to an end,' she said stoically, knowing it was far too soon for her.

Jack raised himself up enough to squint down at her. 'Who says it's the end?'

Ellie rested her chin on his chest and looked at him regretfully, determined to play it cool. 'My boss. I only had two weeks' holiday and most of that has gone already. I'll be flying home in a few days.'

'Is there some law I haven't heard of that says we can't continue seeing each other back in England?' he countered and Ellie was so surprised, she forgot to breathe for a second or two. Then she tried to act calm, though her heart was racing like fury.

'But once we leave here, the pretence will be over,' she reminded him, and he shook his head sadly.

'Funny, but it's all felt very real to me.'

Ellie grimaced, for it was very real to her too, only... 'You know what I mean. This was an act for Luke's benefit.'

'Luke has nothing to do with it. I still want you. Or are you saying you don't want me?' His blue eyes were suddenly narrowed and watchful.

'Of course I want you,' Ellie exclaimed, her mood lifting as she realised it didn't have to be over yet.

'Then that's settled,' Jack declared with satisfaction, and he lay back down again.

Ellie gave herself a mental shake, taking it all in. The relief was heady. It wasn't over. Jack wanted their affair to continue. Happiness bubbled up inside her. She felt like laughing, but bit it back. There was time. Time for what, exactly, she couldn't say. She only knew that far from being the end, this was only the beginning.

Ellie sat in the stern and watched Jack as he kept the yacht headed into the wind. They needed to make up time because they hadn't started on the homeward journey as early as Jack intended. She smiled to herself. It had been his own fault. He shouldn't have kissed her like that. One thing had led to another and, hey presto, it had been closer to lunch than breakfast when they set off.

He was very easy on the eye, and just watching him brought a smile to her lips and a warm glow to her chest.

He was just about perfect, she supposed, and that was probably why she loved him so much.

The thought just slipped into her consciousness with all the force of a hurricane. Ellie was staggered by it. Loved him? She loved him? The world seemed a little unsteady but it had nothing to do with the swell. She couldn't love Jack—could she? The answer came back loud and clear. She could. She did.

Everything she felt, everything that had happened between them, pointed to the truth of it. I love him, she told herself silently and, in the saying, all the things she had been feeling coalesced into a huge swell of emotion inside her. Her heart lurched, then raced on, and she pressed faintly trembling fingers to her lips. Of course she loved him. It was the only thing that made sense.

She could see it now very clearly. He was her destiny. All of her life had been leading to this moment. She loved him—had fallen in love with him there on the dock, when he had appeared to her out of the heat haze.

'Jack.' His name was little more than a breath on the breeze.

No wonder she hadn't wanted this affair to be over. It was because she was in love with him. He had, without her knowing it, become the centre of her world. Everything which was good in her life was connected to him. No other men had been able to make her feel what he had made her feel, because she hadn't loved them. It was Jack. Only Jack.

And then she remembered the woman he loved.

Ellie felt as if she had had heaven within her grasp and had just had it snatched away. She might well love Jack, but he could not love her. His heart belonged to another, and the irony was that part of what made her love him was his steadfast heart. The very thing she loved him for, would keep him from loving her.

Her heart started to ache with an unquenchable pain. As she sat there in the grip of something approaching despair, she knew it wouldn't take much for it to break in two. For to love Jack was to want all of him, and yet she better than anyone knew there was one part of him she could never have—his heart.

Had it been anyone else she might have hoped one day to win his love, but not with Jack. The most he would ever have to offer was affection. At the present, so far as he was concerned, all that was between them was a powerful sexual attraction. If it lasted, he might want a more permanent relationship, but the odds were against it. In all these years he hadn't found anyone he wanted to spend the rest of his life with. Why should she prove any different to the rest? Which left her with only what they had now—for as long as it lasted.

Could she accept that? Did she have any choice? Something always had to be better than nothing, but would a small amount of something fill the void of a whole future with nothing? It would have to, for the alternative was unthinkable. She wouldn't walk away from him. In fact, she doubted that she could do it. He would have to tell her to go. Only then would it finally be over.

'Come back, Ellie,' Jack's gentle command broke through the wall of her thoughts and she blinked at him.

'What?' she asked vaguely then, seeing the concern in his eyes, her heart turned over.

Jack was still frowning. 'You looked lost and sad,' he observed, and Ellie felt colour wash into her cheeks, for that was exactly how she had been feeling.

Licking her lips nervously, she produced a smile, though it was a travesty of the real thing. 'Was I?'

He nodded. 'What were you thinking?'

She shrugged diffidently. 'Oh, that life can play tricks on you.'

'The thing with life is that sometimes you have to look it squarely in the eye and dare it to do its worst,' Jack advised. 'Things have a way of turning out for the best then.'

Her smile widened a little. 'You're speaking from experience? Did it work?'

He grinned. 'The jury's still out, but I've a gut feeling they'll find in my favour.'

Ellie swallowed a painful lump in her throat. 'I hope they do, Jack. I really hope they do.'

For a moment he said nothing, merely looked at her, then he held out a hand to her. 'Come over here. You're too far away and I want to hold you.'

Putting her gloomy thoughts aside, Ellie went to him. 'The last time you held me, we lost all track of time,' she reminded him of just that morning.

Jack pulled her in front of himself so that his arms were around her even as he held the wheel. 'I'll be on my best behaviour. The last thing I want to do is capsize the boat and lose you just when I've caught you.'

Ellie laughed as he intended her to, but unseen by him her eyes glittered with unshed tears. She didn't want him to lose her either, but she knew that fate, that fickle creature, still had its last cards to play.

The party was going with a swing. Everyone was having a wonderful time. At least, all the guests were.

From her position by the window Ellie could see that

Andrea was looking bored, whilst Luke had barely spoken a word. So much for being 'The Happy Couple',
she thought wryly. Not that she was in much of a party
mood herself, but at least she was making an effort to
enjoy herself.

She had spent most of the early evening helping in
the kitchen. Jack and his father had been in charge of
making room for dancing and seeing there were enough
chairs for those who wanted to sit down. Consequently
she had seen very little of him. Which had given her
time to put things in perspective. The sky hadn't fallen
in just because she'd discovered she loved Jack. It was
one of those things she had to have the grace to accept.
Railing against it certainly wasn't going to get her anywhere. In the meantime, she was going to make the most
of what she did have.

Starting right now.

She looked for Jack and found him talking to her
mother. He looked devastatingly handsome in his dinner
suit. Not to mention downright sexy. The music playing
was slow, and she could think of nothing she'd rather
be doing than slowly circling the dance floor in his arms.

The thought being father to the deed, she began to
make her way towards him, but someone walked directly
into her path, forcing her to stop. Stepping back, Ellie
found herself staring into Luke's angry eyes. He was the
very last person she wanted to be talking to, and her first
instinct was to attempt to step round him.

'Excuse me,' she said coolly, but he quickly stepped
in front of her again.

'Not so fast,' he commanded. 'I want to talk to you.
Let's dance.'

Ellie stood her ground. 'I don't think we've anything

to say to each other, and all things considered, I'd rather dance with a toad than you. So, if you don't mind…'

Luke's smile appeared but failed to reach his eyes. 'Oh, but I do mind. I mind about a lot of things. For instance, I mind very much about you and my brother getting all cosy.'

She had known he would. Luke was a sore loser. 'Our relationship has nothing to do with you, Luke,' she told him firmly.

'It is when I find him poaching on my territory. I won't have it, and I intend to put a stop to it,' Luke declared nastily, and Ellie's stomach lurched, for she knew he was a dangerous man to cross.

Still, she wasn't about to show he was making her anxiety level hit the roof. 'Oh, yes, and just how do you plan to do that?' she challenged scornfully, and he smiled.

'Come outside with me and I'll tell you,' he proposed, and Ellie debated whether to comply or not. She didn't want to but she needed to know his intentions.

Shrugging as if the whole business was unimportant, she nodded. 'Very well, I'll listen.'

His amusement was far from encouraging. 'Thought you might,' he mocked, and taking her by the arm led her out onto the terrace. Several people were chatting outside, but off to the left there was a private area. Luke headed for it.

Ellie turned on him then, trying to shake off his hand but he held on and placed his other hand on her shoulder, successfully trapping her. Unwilling to create a scene with others nearby, she was forced to grit her teeth and bear it. 'You had something to tell me,' she reminded him.

'Ah, yes, my brother,' he murmured, allowing his hands to glide down her arms and up again.

His touch made her flesh crawl and she tensed, bristling. 'Stop that!'

'Prefer other hands now, do we?' Luke sneered. 'Just what did you and Jack get up to on that boat?'

Ellie finally managed to prise his hands away by dint of digging her nails in—hard. 'Keep your hands to yourself in future. I'm not your property. I never was. Leave us alone, Luke.'

'Do you love him, Funny Face?' Luke asked, then proceeded to answer his own question. 'Of course you do. You're here right now because you're worried that I might hurt him, aren't you?'

She stared into his angry eyes and knew trouble was brewing. She just didn't know what form it would take. 'I won't let you hurt him,' she warned icily.

He laughed. 'Ah, the power of love. Well, relax, I'm not going to do anything to Jack. He's my brother after all. But you, Ellie, you aren't family at all. You shouldn't have left me, you know. It made me angry, and I really can't let you get away with it.'

Her chin went up, though her heart quailed at the thought of what he could do. He was a very vindictive man. 'You can't do anything to me, Luke.'

'Oh, yes I can. I can take away the one thing you really want. My brother. Call it tit for tat. If I can't have you, then I intend to see Jack doesn't have you either. Perfect.'

If he thought that, he didn't know his brother very well. Jack wasn't easily swayed by outside forces. Knowing it, Ellie shook her head. 'You won't succeed,' she said confidently.

'Care to put a bet on it?'

'You're missing the point. He doesn't love me.' Though it hurt to say it, her defence was strengthened by the truth of it.

To her surprise Luke threw back his head and laughed. 'No, it's you who's missing the point, Funny Face.'

She frowned. 'What do you mean?' A knot settled in her stomach.

'A funny thing happened whilst you were gone. I was out here on the terrace and just happened to overhear a conversation between our parents. Do you want to know what I heard?'

'Not particularly,' she denied, though her heart rate had increased along with a feeling of dread. He was going to tell her, and intuition told her she wasn't going to like it.

'I'll tell you anyway. The parents were talking about you and Jack, and you'll never guess what?'

Ellie gritted her teeth, hating the amusement he was getting from this. 'Either tell me or shut up. I'm not interested in your mean little games, Luke.'

'You'll be interested in this one. Remember the woman I told you Jack had fallen for all those years ago? Brace yourself, darling. Turns out it was you!'

He couldn't have handed her a more profound shock. Ellie stared at him uncomprehending for what seemed like aeons, but was barely a second in reality. She could feel the blood leaving her cheeks as the stunning message got through. 'What did you say?' she asked incredulously.

Luke was enjoying himself. 'I know. Hard to take in, isn't it. You're the mystery woman. Jack loves you. But what you have to ask yourself is this, will he still love you when I tell him about us? Hmm? What do you think?'

Ellie felt the ground sway under her feet. Jack loved her? Had loved her for years? It couldn't be true. She knew it couldn't, and yet... So many things suddenly began to make sense. Things which, separately, meant nothing, but put together pointed to one thing. That Luke was telling the truth. He had no reason to make it up, for as the truth it had untold power. Power to cause pleasure and pain. For whilst there was nothing she wanted to hear more than that Jack loved her, she had no way of knowing how he would react to the news of her affair with Luke.

'Ellie?'

Jack's voice saying her name made Ellie spin round. She could feel his eyes on her face and knew she looked as pale as she felt.

'Hey, Jack!' Luke greeted his brother cheerily. 'We were just talking about you.'

Jack didn't smile as he came closer, for he would have to be an insensitive clod not to pick up on the atmosphere. 'What's going on here?' he demanded to know, looking from one to the other questioningly.

The question was all the opening Luke would need and, recognising that, Ellie pulled herself together in a hurry. At all costs she had to prevent Luke from carrying out his threat. Which meant getting Jack away from there fast. Hurrying to his side, she took his arm.

'Nothing's going on. Let's go back inside,' she urged, mentally willing him to do as she wanted, but Jack didn't move.

Freeing himself, he took Ellie by the shoulders, compelling her to meet his eyes. 'You're lying. You're as white as a sheet. What did he say to you?'

Silently, grey eyes begged him to let them leave. 'Nothing important. Please, Jack, I want to go back now.'

'Don't run away on my account,' Luke put in mockingly, and Ellie shot him a look of pure scorn.

'You're despicable,' she said coldly. Licking her lips nervously, she turned back to Jack. He was looking grim, and her nerves jangled. 'If you come with me, I'll tell you what you want to know, but we have to go now,' she insisted, and could feel the tension in Jack's arm.

He gave her one final look, then took a deep breath and nodded. 'Very well.'

Ellie breathed a sigh of relief as they turned to go back inside, but it was short-lived.

'By the way, Jack,' Luke spoke to their backs. 'You never told me how good she was,' he drawled, and Ellie caught her breath in a horrified gasp.

Jack slowly faced his brother, a deep frown creasing his forehead. 'What was that?'

Luke grinned. 'I wondered how good she was. Just idle curiosity, seeing as I was the one who taught her all she knows. From what I can remember, as lovers go, she was hot!'

Beneath her fingers, Jack went utterly still. 'Say that again,' he commanded in a voice so frosty, Ellie shivered.

Luke was enjoying himself too much to take heed of the undercurrents. 'Didn't she tell you we were lovers? Tut, tut, Ellie, you really should have told him. She was an enthusiastic learner. In fact—'

What he would have said then was a matter for pure

speculation, for at the precise instant Jack knocked him down with one powerful punch. As his brother crumpled at his feet, Jack turned and looked at Ellie. He didn't say a word, but he didn't have to, his silence was eloquent. Ellie's heart twisted painfully in her chest.

Finally he raked a hand through his hair, and shook his head slowly. 'Any denials?'

She swallowed painfully. 'No.'

Spinning on his heel, he went to walk away, pausing beside her for a second. 'He was right about one thing. You should have told me,' he said, then brushed past her and disappeared inside.

Ellie stared after him helplessly, knowing she had been a fool. She had done everything wrong, and now she didn't know if she could put it right. She shivered, feeling cold despite the balmy night air. Of course she was going to try, because she loved him. This was not the time to be faint-hearted. He deserved the truth, no matter how bad it made her appear. Then maybe, if he loved her as Luke said he did, he would understand and forgive her. Lord, she hoped so, because if he didn't, Luke would have his victory.

She gave Luke's unconscious figure one last look, then hurried after Jack. As luck would have it, she bumped into Andrea in the doorway.

'Have you seen Luke?' the other woman asked, in that superior tone that instantly put Ellie's back up. In no mood to suffer in silence, she nodded her head towards the terrace.

'You'll find him out there. Throw a bucket of water over him and give him a couple of aspirin. Then when he's feeling better, ask him what he did to make Jack knock him down. It will make interesting listening!'

With a tight smile she left Andrea gaping and made her way through the gyrating dancers to where her mother and Tom were having an animated conversation by the door.

'Have you seen Jack?' she asked without preamble, and Tom Thornton hiked a thumb towards the stairs.

'He went through here looking like a thundercloud. Last I saw of him he was taking the stairs two at a time.'

'Have you two argued?' her mother asked, searching her face for clues, and Ellie winced.

'Not exactly,' she squirmed, then looked apologetically at her stepfather. 'You might want to go outside and see how Luke is,' she advised, and his brows shot up questioningly. 'Jack hit him,' she elucidated, and drew gasps from the pair of them. Then, to her surprise, Tom started to laugh.

'Well, that's been a long time coming. No doubt Luke deserved it. He must have said something pretty nasty to stir Jack to violence,' he said, and looked another question.

Ellie braced herself, but didn't flinch from telling the truth. 'You might as well know. Luke told Jack we'd been lovers, and Jack took exception to it,' she explained, and met her mother's eyes briefly before glancing away.

'Oh, Ellie!' Mary Thornton exclaimed softly.

Ellie shrugged diffidently. 'Not my only mistake, but the biggest.' By saying it out loud, the enormity hit her hard, and her bottom lip showed an alarming tendency to quiver. She pressed her lips together hard to stop it. 'Trouble is, I know I never did love Luke, but I do love Jack. Which is why I have to go after him and try to explain. Do you think… No, don't answer that. I'll know either way soon enough,' she said with an expressive grimace and headed for the stairs.

Ellie approached Jack's bedroom door with a hollow feeling in her stomach. This was not an interview she was looking forward to, but it had to be done. She knew he had a right to be angry with her, but if he loved her… That was the hope she clung on to as she knocked on the door. Without waiting for an answer, she opened the door and stepped inside, closing it firmly behind her.

Jack lay on the bed, his jacket and tie discarded, shirt sleeves rolled up to the elbow and several buttons opened at his throat. He looked round as the door opened but said nothing until she closed it behind her.

'You weren't invited in,' he told her bluntly.

Ellie rested back against the solid wood and took a deep breath. 'I knew better than to wait for an invitation. You're angry,' she observed and he laughed hollowly.

'Hell, yes, I'm angry. Which is why you shouldn't be here right now,' he shot back, eyes glittering a warning.

'You won't hurt me,' she returned simply and he glared at her.

'Really? Didn't you just see me floor my brother?'

'You were provoked,' she countered, and Jack laughed.

'And you think you aren't provoking me? I don't want you here, so I'd advise you to get out whilst I still have control of my temper,' he ordered, looking away from her.

Ellie held her ground. 'I came to explain about everything, and I'm not leaving until I have.'

'And if I don't want to hear it?' he charged, angry eyes swinging back to her face.

That was the problem. If he really didn't want to hear

anything she had to say, all he had to do was get up and leave. She wouldn't be able to prevent him. She had to say something that would make him stay and hear her out. Whatever it was, it had to be bold, and she had to think of it fast.

'Will you at least tell me why you're so angry?'

Jack came to his feet in one lithe movement and rounded the bed to face her. 'I'm angry, Angel, because I thought you had more sense than to sleep with my brother!'

'Obviously I'm not as bright as you thought I was!' she said gruffly.

A muscle in his jaw clenched. 'You were clever enough to tell the whole family a pack of lies.'

'I know, but there were reasons.'

Jack dragged a hand through his hair. 'There always are. Look, I really don't care to hear about it right now.'

Her nerves jangled as she realised he was about to end the discussion. These were desperate times and called for desperate measures. She knew of only one thing she could say to make him listen. It could open her up for more heartache than she had ever experienced, but she could see no other way.

'You're right, I was a fool, but at least my relationship with Luke taught me what love wasn't, so that I could recognise the real thing when it came along. And it did come along. If you won't let me tell you anything else, at least hear this. I love you, Jack,' she admitted in a voice thick with emotion, and held her breath for his answer.

The confession stunned him into silence for a moment or two, then he gave his head a shake. 'What was that?'

Ellie swallowed hard and kept hold of her courage. 'I

said I love you. It probably won't help, but I just wanted you to know.'

Jack's hands settled on his hips as he looked at her incredulously. 'Damn you, Ellie, you certainly know how to pick your moment!'

She spread her hands in entreaty. 'All I want is a chance to explain.'

He grimaced and rubbed a hand around his neck as if to ease out the kinks. 'OK, I'll listen, though I don't know what you hope to gain.'

She could have told him in a few short words. What she hoped for was that he would tell her he loved her. That at least would tell her all was not lost. What she would settle for... Well, that would depend on the outcome of the next half-hour.

CHAPTER TEN

Now that she had been given the opportunity to explain her actions, Ellie found she didn't exactly know where to start. Jack had walked over to the open window and was staring out into the night sky, his hands shoved into the pockets of his trousers. He looked distant and unapproachable, and those icy fingers tightened their grip on her heart.

From some way away they could still hear the sounds of the party going on downstairs. It seemed to be mocking them.

'Cat got your tongue?' Jack taunted from across the room, and she jumped, realising she was wasting precious time.

She took a couple of hesitant steps towards him, then stopped again. 'I was wondering where to begin,' she confessed.

He laughed humourlessly. 'Trying to work out which version of the events will get the best results?'

That stung, as it was clearly meant to, but at least it had her chin lifting. 'There is only one version—the truth,' she told him firmly, and he shot her a mocking look over his shoulder.

'But with you being such an adept liar, Angel, how am I to know the truth is the truth, hmm?'

That brought colour to her cheeks, for she knew she had made things difficult for herself by all the lies she had told, and then perpetuated. 'I guess I deserve that.

All I can do is tell you the truth as I believe it to be, and let you use your own judgement.'

'This being the judgement that believed you the first time, and has clearly been proved faulty,' he jibed, quirking one lazy eyebrow at her.

Ellie stared at him, knowing she deserved to be given a hard time, but hurting anyway. 'You're determined to make it difficult.'

'Give me one good reason why I should make it easy?' he countered, and she bit her lip.

There was a good reason—because he loved her—but she wouldn't use it. She couldn't use against him something he hadn't told her himself. She believed it to be the truth but, until he said it in as many words, it simply didn't exist. It hadn't come from his heart.

Folding her arms to hide the fact that her hands carried a visible tremor, Ellie crossed the floor to the window and looked out.

'I'm sorry,' she apologised in a soft voice made thick with emotion. 'I never meant to hurt anyone. I just didn't want you all to know how stupid I'd been. It seemed…easier to say nothing. The crazy thing is, the affair didn't even last long. I knew I'd made a mistake almost from the beginning. You remember I told you I'd lost those rose-tinted glasses I'd worn for so long? Well, you don't know how much I wish I'd lost them a lot earlier,' she admitted ruefully. She could feel Jack's eyes on her, but resisted the urge to look round. 'I never knew how selfish Luke was. How incapable he was of being faithful, and how much he enjoyed playing games and manipulating people.'

'It's his favourite pastime,' Jack observed grimly.

She nodded, knowing it now. 'That's what he was doing last Christmas.'

'You were lovers then?' he asked in disbelief, and she nodded.

'Yes.'

'My God!' Jack gritted through his teeth and she knew he was remembering what had happened then.

'Believe me, I had no idea until you told me that he'd asked everyone's advice on what to do about me. You see, he'd insisted we kept the affair secret. At first I thought it was because he didn't want to share what we had with anyone, and that was fun. But then I realised he was never going to say anything. He thought it was a great joke to lead you all down the garden path, and because I'd agreed to it in the first place, I was trapped. I went along with it, but I hated making fools of you all. I just didn't know how to put things right so I decided to say nothing.'

'Something of a habit of yours,' he responded sardonically, and Ellie glanced round at him.

'I hated myself for being used, and for letting down the people I cared about. I knew I'd disappointed you all, and that made me a coward. I've had to live with it, and believe me I'm not proud of myself.'

If she hoped to see a softening of his expression, she was disappointed. Jack's face could have been carved from stone. She had no idea what he was thinking. Confession was good for the soul, and she was glad she was telling him now, but it was doing nothing for her heart.

'So,' Jack said coldly. 'Having discovered what a louse my brother really is, what did you do next?'

Ellie looked at him steadily. 'I ended the affair of

course,' she replied, and at last saw something flicker in the depths of his blue eyes.

'That couldn't have gone down well. Luke prefers to be the one in control,' he observed, and Ellie shrugged.

'It was another thing we disagreed on. Needless to say he didn't accept it. He still thinks he can get me back with a click of his fingers! I've done everything but take out an ad in the newspapers to make him understand it's over. I don't want him. I certainly never loved him. I was Trilby to his Svengali for too many years, but the magic eventually wore off, and I saw him for what he was.'

'Ah, now I understand your change of heart the other day. So you finally decided to use me to prove to him that you didn't want him, didn't you?' he charged, fixing her with a gimlet eye, and she knew she hadn't done her cause any favours.

'It seemed appropriate to try and kill two birds with one stone,' she expanded, but Jack looked sceptical.

'The only trouble with that, Angel, was that there was really only one bird so far as you were concerned. You must have found it vastly amusing to have me insist on you proving to everyone that you had finally got over your crush when you planned to do it all along!' he returned scornfully, and Ellie grimaced, knowing she had been right about how much her behaviour would hurt her family.

She looked at him with regret. 'I never laughed at you, Jack. I used the situation, that was all. You were using it too, remember and you were the one that suggested everything in the first place!'

'At least I was open about my intentions,' he pointed out, and Ellie shook her head at the double standard.

'So it's honourable for you to try and get me into bed, but not for me to have an affair with your brother?' she argued, only to have Jack come right back.

'Everyone could see what I was doing. You and Luke made a point of hiding it. You lied to us. You played us all for fools, and that isn't something we're going to forgive you for too easily.'

That was what she was afraid of. It would be bad enough coming from her mother, but what she really feared was that Jack would not forgive her. 'Surely I'm allowed one foolish mistake?'

Jack's laugh was mirthless. 'True, but you made two. The first one was to get involved with Luke in the first place. The other was lying about it,' he counted off on his fingers, and Ellie felt her heart constrict.

'So you'll allow me the foolishness of falling for Luke, but not the other? I thought you would be kinder.'

Jack's eyes flashed angrily. 'Unluckily for you, Angel, I'm not feeling too kindly right now.'

She should have expected that. 'And what I said makes no difference?' she simply had to ask.

Something glittered in Jack's eyes as he folded his arms and stared down at her. 'You've said quite a lot, so you'd better remind me what you consider significant.'

Ellie caught her breath, discovering for herself that it was impossible to take a pound of flesh without drawing blood. 'I told you I loved you,' she reminded him huskily.

'Oh, that,' he said carelessly. 'Tell me, is there any reason why it should mean anything? It isn't as if the feeling is reciprocated, now is it? Or did you think that because I'd taken you to bed, I loved you?' he went on, and tutted. 'Come on, sweetheart, you should know from your own experience it's possible to sleep with someone without loving them.'

Only then did she truly appreciate just how angry he was. If she told him that she knew he loved her, she would only make things worse. Right now the last thing he wanted her to know was how he felt about her. She would have to hope that in a few days he would see things differently. He would come round in the end. She had to believe that or the future would look incredibly bleak.

Licking trembling lips, she rubbed her hands over her arms uneasily and began to move towards the door. 'I see. In that case I won't disturb you any longer. Thank you for listening to me.' She reached the door but kept her back to him, afraid he would see the gleam of tears in her eyes. 'Will you at least do one thing for me?' she asked as she opened the door.

'Depends what it is,' he responded shortly.

'Just remember I do love you, Jack. Goodnight.'

She didn't wait for a response, but went out and closed the door behind her. Unable to take another step, she pressed a hand to her mouth to hold back a sob. Oh, God, he was so angry, and it was the kind of anger that could make him steel his heart against her. It was possible to push love to its limits, to where forgiveness was impossible. Had she done that? Had she destroyed the one thing that really mattered to her? She really feared that she just might have done.

The thought of rejoining the party right now made her wince, so she walked the few metres to her own room. There was enough light from the moon to illuminate the room, so she didn't bother to switch on the light, merely kicked off her shoes and made herself comfortable on the bed.

What a mess. How had things become so complicated? There was no simple answer, nor a simple solution. Either Jack would come around or he wouldn't. He was angry with her, and he had a right to be. She shouldn't have lied in the first place. But what was done was done. Now all she could do was wait and hope. Never the two easiest things to do, but if there was an alternative, she didn't know about it.

It was going to be a very long night.

Having taken for ever to fall asleep, Ellie woke late the following morning feeling less than refreshed. Her first instinct was to go to Jack, but she knew that would be a mistake. She had to give him time. Steeling herself to what lay ahead, she showered and dressed in a cool cotton sun dress and headed downstairs to face the family. By now everyone would know the main details, but she knew she would have some explaining to do.

Paul was in the kitchen raiding the fridge when she stopped off there to get a cup of coffee. He grinned when he saw her.

'Some party!' he teased, deciding on a chicken drumstick left over from yesterday.

Ellie shuddered and poured herself the coffee. 'I'd rather not think about it.'

'For what it's worth, I'm on your side. Someone should have given Luke a black eye a long time ago.'

Her face mirrored her surprise. 'He has a black eye?'

'A real beauty. Jack sure didn't pull his punch any. I wish I'd seen it.'

His grin was infectious, and Ellie couldn't help laughing. 'He did go down as if he was poleaxed. Mind, it wasn't funny at the time.'

'I guess not. Anyway, it had one result. Luke and Andrea left right after the party, and I can't say I was sorry to see them go. He's a pain and she's a pill. They ought to do well together!' Paul added with a roll of his eyes. 'You'll find Mum and Dad out on the terrace.'

'I'd better go and make my peace with them. Why do I feel about ten years old?'

Paul wagged the half-eaten drumstick at her. 'The price of a guilty conscience. Try grovelling, that generally works.'

Ellie thanked him for the advice and they parted company. She found her mother and Tom where Paul said they would be, but there was no sign of Jack. She didn't know if that was a good sign or not.

'Good morning,' she greeted, kissing them both on the cheek before taking a chair opposite them. 'I hear Luke and Andrea have gone. I'm sorry if what happened caused problems for you.'

Tom Thornton amazed her by looking amused. 'It didn't. Most of our friends were intrigued by the unexpected fight. We could probably dine out on it for the next six months.'

Ellie smiled as she was supposed to do, but her eyes sought her mother's and saw the questions there. 'I guess Jack told you everything,' she sighed, and was surprised when her mother shook her head.

'He hasn't said a word. Other than to say it was up to you to explain.'

That was unexpected but, on consideration, she probably should have guessed. Jack was never one to tell tales. 'Then I'll start at the beginning. Just keep in mind that your daughter is a fool, OK.' So saying she started to tell the whole story about her involvement with Luke, and all the lies she had told. It wasn't a pleasant tale to tell, but it was cathartic. At the end she felt better, if still guilty.

'I don't come out of it very well, do I?' she said ruefully.

'Luke comes off worse. I had no idea my son could be quite that devious,' Tom declared grimly. 'No wonder he left in such a hurry. He knew the truth was bound to come out, and he didn't want to face the music. Never mind. I'm a patient man. I'll catch up with him eventually, and I will have a thing or two to say that he definitely isn't going to like.'

Ellie reached across the table to take his hand. 'I didn't tell you to put all the blame on him. I was at fault too. I'm sorry.'

'No wonder Jack was furious,' Mary Thornton said with a frown. 'He wouldn't have been expecting Luke's confession.'

Which brought Ellie to something important she wanted to ask. She sat forward and chose her words carefully. 'There was one other thing that Luke said, and I need to know if he told the truth. I think he did, but only you can confirm it. He said that Jack loved me. He had overheard the two of you talking about us, and that you said I was the mystery woman he was in love with. Is it true? Please tell me. I have to know.'

Mary gave her husband a significant look. 'I told you I thought I heard someone outside,' she tutted. Turning back to her daughter, she sighed. 'There doesn't seem to be much point in denying it, does there? Yes, Jack loves you, and he's waited a long time for you. This thing with Luke…well, it must have been a blow. And now you know you love Jack, who I've always thought was the perfect man for you, and it's all blown up in your face. Ellie, my darling, you do make things difficult for yourself.'

Ellie smiled ruefully. 'I know. But I told him I love him, and I'm hoping that soon he'll stop being angry with me. Then perhaps he'll admit he loves me. I need him to tell me.'

Her mother's brows rose. 'He doesn't know you know, does he?' she exclaimed in surprise, and Ellie shook her head.

'No. I couldn't do that to him. If he wants me to know, he'll tell me. If not…' she left that hanging. If he didn't want her to know. If he couldn't forgive her deception, then it didn't make any difference what she knew. Love had to be unconditional. Freely given and freely returned, otherwise it meant nothing.

There was a look of pride in Mary's eyes. 'That's very brave of you, darling.'

Ellie shook her head. 'I'm not brave, I'm terrified, but I love him enough to let him go, if what happened has pushed him too far. I made a fool of him, and that hurts a man's pride.'

'Pride is all very well, but it can't hold you and love you, and keep you warm at night,' Tom argued. 'Which I will be happy to point out to him the next time I see him.'

'Tom!' Mary cautioned much too late. Sighing, she looked ruefully at her daughter.

Ellie's heart lurched. 'When you see him? But, I thought… Where is Jack?' she demanded in sudden alarm.

'He left on the first ferry this morning. We did try to make him change his mind, but he was adamant.'

Ellie glanced at her watch and closed her eyes helplessly. He had been gone hours. He would be almost back in England by now. Swallowing hard, she smiled wanly. 'Well, that's that then.'

'Darling it doesn't mean he's made a decision, just that he had to get away for a while. You have to keep your chin up,' her mother said reassuringly, worry written plainly on her face.

Ellie did her best not to look downhearted. 'I bet you're right, but if it's all the same with you, I think I'll go home too.' There really didn't seem to be any point in staying if Jack had gone.

'You must do what you think best, darling,' Mary comforted. 'We'd love to have you stay longer, but if you must go, then so be it.'

'Would you like me to make the arrangements?' Tom offered, and Ellie nodded gratefully. He went off to use the telephone, and Ellie was left facing her mother.

'I'd better go and pack,' she said, getting to her feet.

Mary smiled at her fondly. 'Don't give up. Jack hasn't loved you this long to lose you now. He'll realise it soon enough.'

Ellie took the thought with her as she went upstairs again. She was going to do her best to look on the bright side, but it wasn't going to be easy. If only Jack were still here she wouldn't feel so ill at ease. Although there was an upside to the situation. At least in England she would be nearer to him, so, if he wanted to get in touch, she wouldn't be hundreds of miles away. But, if he didn't call, a few miles would feel like a hundred to her heart.

*   *   *

London was basking in a mini-heatwave. Normally heat didn't bother Ellie, but this time she found it enervating. She had been home for two weeks now, and had heard nothing from Jack. The heat was making it hard for her to keep her hopes up. She kept telling herself fourteen days was no time at all, but as each day passed her heart ached a little more.

Ellie couldn't count the number of times she had actually picked up the phone, intending to call Jack, only to put it down again with the number half punched-in. She longed to hear his voice, but had promised herself she would not pressure him. He had to come to her. It had to be his decision.

Today she had arrived home from work feeling limp and drained. The job she was working on was more intricate than most, and for some reason she had been all fingers and thumbs, so that she had had to unpick what she had done several times. In then end she had decided to call it quits for the day, and hope that tomorrow her concentration would be back.

Her first task when she arrived home, as always, had been to check the answer phone and her computer for messages, but there were none. Dispirited, she had showered and slipped into an old baggy T-shirt, then padded into the tiny kitchen of her flat and glanced through the meagre contents of her fridge. Nothing tempted her, but she made herself eat a yoghurt. Her appetite had vanished along with Jack.

Flicking on the TV, she listened to the news, which all seemed to be depressing, then surfed desultorily through the channels, trying to find something that would occupy her mind. The telephone rang, and she reached for it automatically.

'Hello,' she greeted, wondering if it could be her mother calling. She had done so several times since Ellie had returned home. When nobody answered immediately, she frowned, not in the mood for crank calls. 'Who is this?' she demanded to know.

'Ellie?' The surprise in the voice at the end of the line had her sitting up like a Jack-in-the-box.

'Jack?' she breathed back, knocked for a loop, but knowing it was his voice. 'Jack is that you?' she asked in a stronger voice when only silence followed her query. She had opened her mouth to say more when she heard the sound of the receiver going down. 'No! Wait!' she called out, but it was too late, the connection was severed.

Ellie stared at the useless lump of plastic in her hand in a state of shock. Jack had called her. No matter that he hadn't said more than one word. No matter that the surprise in his tone suggested that he hadn't intended to call her. Something had directed his fingers to punch in her number. Could he be as lonely and miserable as she was? Could he secretly want to contact her but his pride was getting in the way?

Her thoughts whirling, Ellie fumbled the receiver back into its rest. Her hands were trembling and she pressed them together to stop it. After two weeks of silence, the sound of his voice had sent her heart soaring. If only he hadn't rung off. If only he would call again. She stared at the phone, willing it to do just that, but it remained stubbornly silent.

Ellie shot to her feet and began pacing the room as the minutes passed and turned into half an hour. This was awful. He had to call again. He just had to. As she approached the phone again, she glared at it.

'Ring, damn you! Ring!' she commanded the silent machine, then positively jumped out of her skin when the front doorbell peeled instead.

Pressing a hand to her wildly thumping heart, Ellie gathered her composure and went to answer the summons. Expecting it to be one of her neighbours come to borrow sugar or coffee, she plastered a smile on her face and opened the door. The smile disappeared when she saw who stood on her doorstep.

Jack's tall, broad-shouldered figure filled the doorway. He was still in the dark suit he must have worn for work, but he carried no briefcase. In fact his hands were stuffed into his trouser pockets, and he was frowning.

'Tell me what the hell I'm doing here,' he growled at her, and Ellie blinked, her jaw dropping at his unexpected arrival, and less than gracious question.

Something told her that if she said the wrong thing, he might just turn and walk away again, so she pulled herself together in a hurry. He clearly needed an answer and, with a mind gone blank, she said the first thing that entered her head.

'You missed me and couldn't stay away a moment longer?' she suggested, then cringed at what had to be the very worst thing she could have said. He was going to leave. He was...

'You got it in one, Ellie,' Jack grunted, surprising her yet again. 'Well, are you going to ask me in?' he charged, staring down at her.

Not sure that she hadn't fallen asleep and was dreaming, Ellie stepped out of his way. 'Come in,' she invited, totally bemused. He stepped round her and headed for her sitting room. Ellie was left to close the door and follow, slowly absorbing the knowledge that he had missed her. Hope fluttered its tiny wings.

She had no idea what was going on, and his mood hardly appeared lover-like, but her heart had leapt at the sight of him and, no matter that he was behaving oddly, she was so very pleased to see him. Jack, meanwhile, was wandering around the room inspecting her books and CD collections. She watched in silence as he picked things up, studied them for a while, then put them back again.

Folding her arms in a protective gesture, Ellie cleared her throat. 'I didn't expect you. I mean, I wanted you to come, but didn't expect you would. After all, it's been two weeks.' The longest two weeks of her life.

'Fifteen days, eleven hours and—' he glanced at his watch '—thirty-seven minutes, to be precise,' he told her.

Her jaw showed a tendency to drop again, and she closed it with a snap. 'You kept count?'

'Didn't you?' he asked, and she nodded, suddenly feeling a great need to smile, but not knowing if she should. Jack removed his jacket and tossed it onto a chair, then proceeded to remove his tie and unbutton the neck of his shirt. 'I intended to stay away longer, but as you can see, here I am.'

A smile did escape her then at the disgust in his voice. 'Yes, here you are,' she agreed softly.

'I've waited for you all this time, so you'd think I could stay away for a few more days!' he railed at himself, and Ellie found her smile turning into a grin. Jack saw it, and his hands settled on his hips as he sighed heavily. 'I know, I know. Unfortunately for my intentions to make you suffer a little longer, I spoke to your mother this evening and she casually informed me that you knew I loved you before you came to plead your case that night. Why didn't you say anything?'

Ellie sobered instantly, though to hear him finally admit that he loved her brought a lump to her throat. 'Because I couldn't do that to you, Jack. Love shouldn't be used as a tool to get what you want from somebody. I want you to love me. It's broken my heart to know I've hurt you and let you down. If I could change it I would, but I can't.'

Jack came to her then, reaching out to cup her face in his hands. 'Thank you for saying nothing. I couldn't have told you I loved you that night because I was too angry, but I can say it now. I love you, Ellie. I've loved you for a long time, and God willing, I intend to love you till the end of for ever,' he said softly but firmly, and the warmth and love in his eyes was suddenly there for her to see.

The declaration brought tears to her eyes. 'So you forgive me?' she asked in a wobbly voice, and he smiled.

'Of course I forgive you, Angel. I love you.'

Ellie closed her eyes, made almost speechless by the emotions welling up inside her. Yet there was one important thing she had to ask him before she could allow herself to believe that everything was going to be all right.

'And Luke?' she probed gruffly. 'Do you mind very much about him?'

Jack sighed and pulled her into the haven of his arms, resting his cheek on her hair. 'I wish he had never been a part of your life, Ellie, but I know he means nothing to you. Like I told you once, the past is another country. We won't go there again.'

Relief made the tears overflow, and for a minute or two Ellie could do nothing to stop them flowing. Eventually though she sniffed and looked up at him. 'Just how long had you intended to make me wait?' she demanded to know in a stronger voice, and Jack had the grace to look shamefaced.

'Another week,' he admitted. 'Although I doubt very much if I would have got beyond tomorrow. I knew I was in trouble when I found myself dialling your number when I meant to order Chinese,' he added wryly, and she laughed.

'Oh, I do love you!' she exclaimed, hugging him tightly.

'Ellie?' Jack's use of her name in that tone made her look up again. 'I'm sorry I put you through hell these last two weeks,' he apologised and she lifted one hand to stroke his cheek.

'I might forgive you in a couple of weeks,' she teased, and brought a glint to his blue eyes that sent shivers down her spine.

'Sooner than that, I hope. I've come to claim my prize,' he told her, and Ellie frowned.

'Prize?'

Jack grinned. 'I bet you, you'd have forgotten all about Luke by the end of the summer. The winner was to name their own prize.'

She remembered, and this was one bet she was happy to lose. 'And just what prize are you claiming?'

'Your hand in marriage just as soon as it can be arranged,' he declared, taking her breath away.

She was so happy she could have burst. 'Is that the only proposal I'm going to get?'

'Take it or leave it,' Jack confirmed, and Ellie threw her arms about his neck and kissed him.

'Oh, I take it! You're mine now, Jack Thornton, and don't you forget it.'

Jack brushed her lips with his. 'I've always been yours, Angel, but now we both know it,' he murmured, and anything more she might have said was lost beneath his lips as he kissed her.

Modern Romance™
...seduction and
passion guaranteed

Tender Romance™
...love affairs that
last a lifetime

Sensual Romance™
...sassy, sexy and
seductive

Blaze.
...sultry days and
steamy nights

Medical Romance™
...medical drama on
the pulse

Historical Romance™
...rich, vivid and
passionate

MILLS & BOON®

Winner at

2001 IDEA
INTERNATIONAL
DESIGN
EFFECTIVENESS
AWARDS

MAT5

GIVE US YOUR THOUGHTS

Mills & Boon® want to give you the best possible read, so we have put together this short questionnaire to understand exactly what you enjoy reading.

Please tick the box that corresponds to how appealing you find each of the following storylines.

32 Richmond Square

They're fab, fashionable – and for rent. When the apartments in this central London location are let, the occupants find amazing things happen to their love lives. The mysterious landlord always makes sure that there's a happy ending for everyone who comes to live at number 32.

How much do you like this storyline?

❑ Strongly like ❑ Like ❑ Neutral – neither like nor dislike
❑ Dislike ❑ Strongly dislike

Please give reasons for your preference:

_____

_____

The Marriage Broker

This city agency matches marriage partners for practical as well as emotional reasons. Upmarket, discreet and with an international clientele, The Marriage Broker offers a personal service to match clients' needs and situations.

How much do you like this storyline?

❑ Strongly like ❑ Like ❑ Neutral – neither like nor dislike
❑ Dislike ❑ Strongly dislike

Please give reasons for your preference:

_____

_____

A Town Down Under

Meet the men of Paradise Creek, an Australian outback township, where temperatures and passions run high. These guys are rich, rugged and ripe for romance – because Paradise Creek needs eligible young women!

How much do you like this storyline?

❏ Strongly like ❏ Like ❏ Neutral – neither like nor dislike
❏ Dislike ❏ Strongly dislike

Please give reasons for your preference:
_____

_____

The Marriage Treatment

Welcome to Byblis, an exclusive spa resort in the beautiful English countryside. None of the guests have ever found the one person who would make their private lives complete…until the legend of Byblis works its magic – and marriage proves to be the ultimate treatment!

How much do you like this storyline?

❏ Strongly like ❏ Like ❏ Neutral – neither like nor dislike
❏ Dislike ❏ Strongly dislike

Please give reasons for your preference:
_____

_____

Name: _____

Address: _____

_____

Postcode: _____

Thank you for your help. Please return this to:

Mills & Boon (Publishers) Ltd
FREEPOST SEA 12282
RICHMOND, TW9 1BR

NO STAMP NEEDED – postage has been paid.

2 FREE

books and a surprise gift!

We would like to take this opportunity to thank you for reading this Mills & Boon® book by offering you the chance to take TWO more specially selected titles from the Modern Romance™ series absolutely FREE! We're also making this offer to introduce you to the benefits of the Reader Service™—

- ★ FREE home delivery
- ★ FREE gifts and competitions
- ★ FREE monthly Newsletter
- ★ Exclusive Reader Service discount
- ★ Books available before they're in the shops

Accepting these FREE books and gift places you under no obligation to buy, you may cancel at any time, even after receiving your free shipment. Simply complete your details below and return the entire page to the address below. *You don't even need a stamp!*

YES! Please send me 2 free Modern Romance books and a surprise gift. I understand that unless you hear from me, I will receive 4 superb new titles every month for just £2.55 each, postage and packing free. I am under no obligation to purchase any books and may cancel my subscription at any time. The free books and gift will be mine to keep in any case.

P2ZEA

Ms/Mrs/Miss/Mr ....Initials......................................

BLOCK CAPITALS PLEASE

Surname ....

Address ....

....

....Postcode...................................

Send this whole page to:
UK: FREEPOST CN81, Croydon, CR9 3WZ
EIRE: PO Box 4546, Kilcock, County Kildare (stamp required)